DEADLY OBSESSION

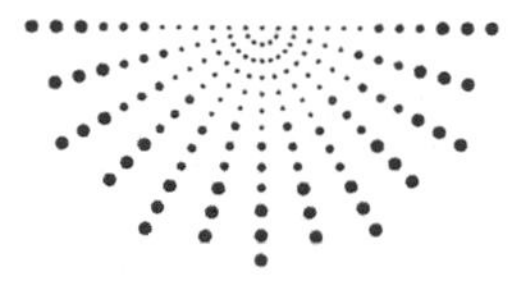

D. S. BUTLER

Deadly Obsession
Deadly Motive
Deadly Revenge
Deadly Justice
Deadly Ritual
Deadly Payback
Deadly Game
Lost Child
Her Missing Daughter
Bring Them Home
Where Secrets Lie

Created with Vellum

DEADLY OBSESSION

DEADLY OBSESSION IS THE first book in the DS Jack Mackinnon Crime Series.

HE WATCHES ... HE WAITS ... HE STRIKES

A young Polish girl fixated on fame. A killer with a deadly obsession.

DS Jack Mackinnon has his work cut out trying to track down missing student, Anya Blonski. As Mackinnon follows the trail of obsession to the shady owners of the Star Academy, who thrive on society's obsession with reality TV shows, he realises the fame they offer comes at a price.

When a second girl goes missing, Mackinnon believes a serial killer is stalking the city.

DEADLY OBSESSION is a British police procedural, perfect for fans of Peter James and his Roy Grace series.

CHAPTER ONE

THE MAN WAITED ON the corner of Queen's street, outside Oakland's Furniture Store.

He took a quick glance at his watch and smiled. Only a few more minutes to go.

Dressed like an American tourist, he blended in with the bustling crowds. He wore a pair of beige, baggy cargo trousers, and a faded, blue, loose cotton shirt with the arms rolled up. His Dodgers baseball cap was pulled down low, and wraparound shades hid his eyes. Despite the setting sun, he kept the glasses on. In London, thousands of CCTV cameras recorded the public's every move, and he didn't want anyone identifying him from the video footage.

He stepped to his right, moving out of the way, as a customer left the furniture store. He studied his reflection in the shiny store windows, hardly recognising himself.

The heat from the pavement seeped up through the soles of his shoes, making his feet hot and uncomfortable.

An expensive video camera hung from a thin, grey, nylon cord around his neck. He looked like just another visitor, taking in the historical sights London had to offer.

His video camera was a premium, state-of-the-art Nikon. He slipped the black cap off the upgraded lens. The zoom lens alone cost him over a thousand pounds. But it was worth it. He needed to get the shot right the first time. There would be no second chances. No reruns.

He raised a hand to his shirt pocket, and his fingers gripped the hard square of the spare memory card. That was good. The one in the camera already contained hours of entertainment, and it wouldn't do to run out of memory today. Not when he had such plans.

He licked his dry lips and closed his eyes. He could hardly bear the anticipation. If only she knew the effect she had on him. But of course, she knew. They all did.

He pointed the video camera at the entrance, so he would be ready when she left the building. His hands trembled so much, the picture in the viewfinder jumped and jerked around. He would have to hold the camera steady with both hands to get a decent recording.

Two women walked past him, city workers dressed in tight skirt suits and the kind of towering shoes that required a desk job. The taller woman glanced at him as she strode past. She tossed her long, brown hair and took a second look, staring at him with obvious curiosity, wondering what he was filming.

Nosy busybody.

The man turned away and pulled out a crumpled packet of Silk Cut cigarettes from his trouser pocket. He didn't want people watching him. He wanted to fade into the background. He had to look like he was just exploring the city. One of many sightseers London saw every day. Then no one would remember him.

It was important to go unnoticed today because if everything went as arranged…

A red, double-decker bus squealed to a halt at the bus stop in front of him.

The man crushed the cigarette in his fist. No! This was not part of the plan.

He watched as passengers clambered off the bus. One, two, three… They kept coming. No! Now there were too many people around. His plan was ruined. The intricate calculations, the careful consideration of possibilities, working out the timing – all for nothing. How could he concentrate with all these people squeezing up against him?

What if one of them remembered him?

"Yes, officer, there was a man lurking around. Of course, I can give you an accurate description…"

No, no, no. It wouldn't do at all.

He shot an anxious glance to the doorway on his right. Any moment now, she would walk through that archway. The culmination of weeks of preparation. It should be the perfect moment. A special moment he would remember for months. A memory he could relive, over and over; but all these people were spoiling it.

White-hot rage blistered in his chest. His hands shook as he tried to pluck another cigarette from the packet. Beads of sweat broke out on his forehead and down the length of his back. He threw the second cigarette on the floor and stamped on it. What was wrong with him? If he wasn't careful, he would ruin the whole thing. He needed to keep calm and stay in control.

It would be all right. If he could just keep a clear head, he might be able to pull it off. The bus pulled away, behind a transit van that belched out diesel fumes; and the passengers were leaving now, clearing a path for him. How considerate. Everything would work out perfectly. He allowed himself a small smile.

The door opened, and he caught his breath.

There she was. Anya. His star.

Her eyes swept over him, then she looked away.

Oh, she was a good actress, pretending not to know him. Pretending she didn't know what was about to happen, as if she hadn't been communicating with him for weeks with those longing looks and secret smiles.

He switched on the video camera, and a blinking red light appeared in the corner of the screen.

How clever of her. She was sending him more signals today. Wasn't she wearing pink? She picked out that soft, rose-coloured cardigan that clung to all her curves just for him. It was a signal, a sign that she was ready, ripe for the plucking. She was telling him she was willing, telling him it had to be today.

Anya turned and began to walk away.

He felt a flash of fire in his chest. Then he took a breath, dispersing the anger, and smiled. Of course, this was all part of the game. She wanted him to follow her.

He would play along. For now. But soon she would realise that *he* made the rules.

He hung back for a few moments; then, with his heart

pounding, he dropped into step behind her, unable to wipe the smile from his face.

He had waited for this moment for so long. He even dreamed about it. But this was no dream. He clenched and unclenched his fists. This was real.

Her long, fair hair tumbled down her back, swaying from side to side as she walked. She pulled off her pink cardigan and tied it around her tiny waist. She wore a bright blue, short skirt, which showed off her long, dancer's legs and rose a little higher with each step. He bit the side of his mouth. He was enjoying the game.

He kept his camera focused on her back, zooming in until she filled the frame.

At first, he stayed a safe distance behind her. From experience, he knew surprise was his best weapon. He followed quietly, a few feet behind her, crossing the road when she did.

She turned right into Bakers Lane. It was quieter here. The traffic from the main road was muffled. He heard the distant ring of church bells and the caw of a crow.

He waited for a moment, looking up and down the street, until he was certain they were alone; then he left the camera dangling from his neck and made his approach.

Hearing his footsteps, she whirled around. Her face was white, pinched and scared.

She put a fluttering hand to her chest and let out a little high-pitched giggle. "You scared me. I didn't realise it was you."

He smiled back at her, walking closer as his hand closed around the knife in his coat pocket.

"Well, I'd better be getting home," she said in her delightful accent.

How sweet! She was still playing the game. His thumb pressed lightly against the sharp edge of the knife.

Her baby blue eyes gazed up at him, wide and trusting.

But why shouldn't she trust him? She knew him, didn't she? At least, she thought she did.

And after tonight, she would know him better than anyone. And he would know every inch of her.

CHAPTER TWO

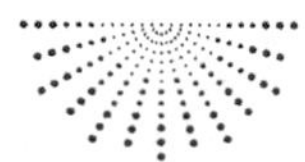

AT EIGHT FIFTEEN ON Wednesday morning, Henryk Blonski, watched the taxi pull up outside his block of flats on the Towers Estate.

After he stopped, the middle-aged taxi driver peered through the insect-splattered windscreen, looking uneasy. Henryk couldn't say he blamed him. It was a horrible area. For the hundredth time this morning, Henryk wondered why he and his sister ever left Poland.

Henryk walked towards the passenger side of the taxi and waited while the driver looked him up and down. The driver's eyes lingered over Henryk's crumpled jeans and t-shirt as well as the stubble on his chin.

Henryk had not had time for a shave this morning. Impatiently, he pushed his dark hair out of his eyes and rapped on the passenger window.

Obviously deciding Henryk looked safe enough, the

driver unlocked the passenger door, and Henryk climbed into the sagging front passenger seat.

"Where to, mate?" the driver asked. His breath smelled of cigarettes and Polo mints.

"Wood Street Police Station," Henryk said.

The driver didn't look surprised by the request, probably assuming residents on this estate had to spend a good deal of time at police stations.

At first, the driver didn't try to engage Henryk in conversation, which was a good thing. Henryk Blonski had other things on his mind.

His sister, Anya, had not come home last night.

Henryk had not noticed she was missing until this morning. He felt his stomach churn. Anya was not the sort of girl to stay out all night. He'd taken a cup of tea into her at seven thirty, as usual, and dropped it on the floor when he saw her bed had not been slept in.

"So whatcha going to see the boys in blue for?" The taxi driver asked as he braked hard at a red light.

Henryk blinked and turned to the driver. Henryk guessed he was in his early sixties. There was a photograph of a couple of small children taped to his dashboard, maybe his children or grandchildren. A family man anyway.

"I'm sorry?" Henryk said.

"The police. Why are you going there?"

Henryk could have told the man to mind his own business, but instead, he bowed his head and said, "My sister. She is missing."

"Missing? I'm sorry to hear that."

Henryk accepted the man's sympathy with a nod.

The driver pulled away from the traffic lights and overtook a single-decker bus without indicating.

"So how long has she been gone?"

"She didn't come home last night."

"Just the one night?" The taxi driver shrugged. "How old is she?"

"Nineteen."

The old man's face relaxed, and he smacked his lips together. "She'll be home, right as rain. She probably just pulled an all-nighter. You know what girls her age are like." The driver gave Henryk a wink.

"My sister is not like that," Henryk said, his voice stiff.

"Well, no," the taxi driver shifted in his seat. "I don't suppose she is. I didn't mean any offence. I hope you find her."

Henryk stayed silent.

"Where are you from?"

"Poland."

The taxi driver was quiet for a moment. He drummed his fingers against the steering wheel. Then suddenly, as if coming to a decision, he turned to Henryk. "A little bit of advice, son, for dealing with the police."

Henryk nodded.

"You've got to handle them right. You need to have them on your side. I can see you're worried, and you're angry, but you need to keep your cool. Do you understand? I used to be a copper, so I know what I'm talking about. They'll want to help you, but they'll have to ask questions about your sister, questions you might not like."

Henryk only half-listened as the taxi driver spoke, his mind focused on what in the world he would tell his mother. How could he tell his parents that Anya was missing?

Henryk gave another curt nod and looked out of the window. Despite staring out at the road, Henryk wouldn't have been able to describe the route the taxi driver took between the Towers Estate and the police station; his thoughts were occupied by what he would tell the police.

He snapped back to the present as the taxi passed St. Alban on Wood Street and pulled up outside the City of London Police Station. He shoved a ten-pound note into the driver's lap and tried to open the door before the car had fully stopped.

"Hold your horses," the driver said.

Henryk ignored him, scrambled out of the car and ran up the stone steps to the entrance, which was flanked by two blue police lanterns. The door was open, and Henryk strode in and told the grey-haired officer behind the desk he needed to talk to someone urgently as his sister was missing.

The officer took down Henryk's name, then started tapping on his computer keyboard. The screen was facing the wrong way, so he couldn't see what the officer was typing.

Henryk looked around the reception area. The station was smaller than he expected. The floor was cream linoleum, and the walls were light grey and covered with posters and notices.

The officer behind the desk handed Henryk a form and nodded to the row of four chairs lined up against the wall on Henryk's right.

Henryk took the form and a black Biro and sat down. At

the end of the narrow reception room was a blue door, with a security panel by the handle. Henryk kept one eye on the door as he filled out the form, expecting a high-ranking officer to come through at any moment. They would want to take down his sister's details as soon as possible.

He filled in the boxes on the form as quickly as he could, printing in capitals because his hand shook as he wrote, and handed it back to the man behind the desk. Then he sat back to wait.

At nine thirty, a group of small children were ushered into the reception area. They were escorted by two women, one short and plump, the other, tall and thin. "Stay together now, children, please. We'll see the police horses next," the tall one said.

After the school children were escorted away on their tour, Henryk looked at his watch. He had been at the station for almost an hour. Anything could have happened to his sister. Anything.

Henryk felt a sharp, stabbing pain behind his right eye. Where was she? Was she hurt? Had there been an accident? Had someone done something to her?

After he couldn't stand to sit any longer, he stood up and paced the narrow room. He looked at the posters for Police Community Support Officers and notices about suspicious packages.

He glared at the man behind the desk, who, oblivious to Henryk's rising anger, smiled back cheerfully.

Henryk wanted to throw something at him. Where was his sister?

He leaned across the reception desk. "I am still waiting. Have you told anyone I am here?"

"Yes, sir. Someone will be down to talk to you shortly."

Henryk sighed heavily before sitting down again and rubbing his eyes. Why was this taking so long?

After another five minutes, the pain behind Henryk's eyes was so bad he could hardly think straight. He was ready to explode.

The blue side door opened, and a man in a shiny suit stepped out. He looked at the officer behind the desk, who nodded at Henryk.

The man in the shiny suit turned to face Henryk and held out his hand. "Henryk Blonski, I'm DC Collins. I understand your sister is missing."

Henryk jumped to his feet. At last!

"Yes. My sister, Anya, did not come home last night. You must understand; this is not like her at all. I think something bad has happened to her."

DC Collins opened the blue door again and ushered Henryk through the entrance.

As DC Collins escorted him through the station, Henryk told him about Anya.

DC Collins didn't speak until they walked inside a small room and he'd shut the door behind them. The furnishings were nicer than in the reception. The floor was carpeted, and the chairs were padded and upholstered, but as Henryk sat down, he barely noticed.

Collins pulled a pen out of his jacket pocket and started to write in his notebook. "So your sister's name is Anya Blonski. How do you spell that?"

Henryk tried hard to hide his irritation. "I already wrote it on the form."

DC Collins waited, his pen poised.

Henryk spelled out her name.

As DC Collins wrote, Henryk watched him with his fists clenched. The detective looked in his mid-thirties. He had a heavy build and short, fair hair. Physically, he seemed built for paperwork, rather than action.

"So you will start looking for her now, yes?" Henryk asked.

"Have you tried calling Anya's mobile?"

Henryk shook his head in disbelief. "Of course, I have. She doesn't answer. I just hear a recorded message saying, *'the mobile you have called has been switched off'*."

"How old is your sister, Mr. Blonski?"

Henryk's knee bounced up and down underneath the table. He'd already written Anya's date of birth on the form. What was the point in filling out these forms if no one looked at them? "She is nineteen."

DC Collins put his pen down on the table, leaned back in his chair and frowned at Henryk. "She has only been missing one night. Perhaps, you're worrying unnecessarily. Maybe she met someone, spent the night with them?"

"Anya is not like that!"

The detective exhaled slowly. Then he asked a succession of horrible questions about Anya. Did she have many men in her life? Was she a drug user?

Henryk was at boiling point. He told DC Collins that Anya had been a straight-A student back in Poland. She was a good girl, only interested in dancing.

The detective listened with a bored look on his face. "Maybe she doesn't tell you everything about her personal life."

Henryk jumped to his feet. DC Collins began to stand,

but Henryk moved faster. He reached over and grabbed the detective by the lapels of his jacket and then shoved him back against the wall. There was a loud thud as DC Collins' head hit the plasterboard.

DC Collins scrambled to his feet as two other officers slammed their way into the room.

"What's going on here?" one of the police officers asked, glaring at Henryk.

DC Collins straightened his tie and his suit jacket. "It's all right. Everything's fine, Leonard. It was just a misunderstanding."

The other officers hovered by the door, but DC Collins waved them off. Then he turned back to Henryk, who was breathing heavily.

"Sit down in that chair now." DC Collins pulled the chair forward. "Do you realise what you just did? Do you want me to arrest you for assaulting a police officer? Do you want to go and personally check out the cells?"

Henryk gritted his teeth. What the hell was the matter with him? He had to calm down. Maybe he misjudged this detective. Maybe he would be able to help. In any case, Henryk didn't have anyone else to turn to. He needed DC Collins' help.

As his fury and adrenaline trickled away, Henryk slumped into the chair. "I'm sorry. I just want you to find Anya."

Collins sat back down and picked up his pen. "Don't you ever behave like that again. Next time, you won't be so lucky. Now, tell me why you think something has happened to your sister."

Henryk tried to explain. He tried to tell the detective

that his sister was not like those other girls. She would not have taken a job abroad without telling him. She had not taken any of her clothes. What normal girl would leave home and not take any clothes?

Despite his best efforts, he could tell DC Collins remained unconvinced. He felt his hope slipping away as the detective gave him statistics, talked about giving her time and told Henryk his sister was behaving like a normal teenager.

But it wasn't normal. Not for Anya.

* * *

Later that day, Detective Sergeant Jack Mackinnon sat in the wide, open plan office at Wood Street Police Station. He was nearing the end of his shift, but rather than looking forward to knocking off for the day, he was dreading it.

His mobile buzzed and vibrated its way along his desk. He looked at it for a second or two, delaying the inevitable, then snatched it up. The message was from Chloe, his girlfriend of just a few months.

See you in an hour x

Mackinnon pulled at the collar of his shirt. He was sweating. He looked at his watch. In an hour, he would be meeting Chloe's kids for the first time. Was it normal to feel this nervous?

A muttered curse made Mackinnon look up. Sitting at the desk opposite, DC Nick Collins hung up his phone before slumping forward with his head in his hands. Collins was in his mid-thirties, close in age to Mackinnon, but unlike Mackinnon, Collins was already married with two kids.

Collins ran a hand over his tightly cropped, fair hair.

"What's up?" Mackinnon asked.

Collins looked up. "Henryk Blonski. He's back in reception. That bloody man won't leave me alone. He only reported his sister missing this morning. He must think I've got magical powers."

"Maybe he wants to tell you that she turned up."

Collins shook his head. "Apparently not. That was Jim Dobson, on the front desk. He said Blonski has taken up residence in reception, and isn't budging until he talks to me and finds out what I am doing to find his sister."

"Do you want me to speak to him? I'll tell him we're working on it, and we'll tell him as soon as we have any news."

Collins dropped his pen on his desk and sighed. "No. It's all right. I'll tell him myself." Collins stood up. "She's only been missing since last night, for God's sake."

"How old is she?"

"Nineteen."

"Suspicious?"

"No more than any other nineteen-year-old who stayed out for the night. It's only been one night. She probably stayed over at a friend's."

"But her brother doesn't think so?"

Collins shrugged. "He seems the overprotective type. I told him people are reported missing all the time and normally show up after a day or two."

Mackinnon nodded. A quarter of a million people were reported missing in the UK every year. Mackinnon looked down at the mobile phone on his desk. These days, with millions of CCTV cameras, registered mobile phones and credit cards, it was hard to believe people could just slip off the radar without anyone noticing, but they did. All the time.

Collins was right. In the majority of cases, the missing person returned of his or her own accord, in their own good time.

"She told a friend she had a new job," Collins said. "To be honest, it sounds like she was just getting a bit sick of her overbearing brother. And I'm starting to share that sentiment. He launched himself at me this morning. All because I suggested she might have a boyfriend she hadn't told him about."

"Are you sure you don't want me to have a word with him? You shouldn't see him on your own if you think he might turn violent."

"He won't. He only went for me this morning because I provoked him. If something has happened to his sister, chances are, it's someone she knew; so I was pressing his buttons, aiming for a reaction. I just got a little more than I bargained for."

Mackinnon nodded. He remembered a case a few years back where a father reported his daughter missing. He was distraught, hysterically accusing anyone who had ever so much as spoken to her. It turned out, he'd strangled her in a fit of rage during an argument over a missing packet of cigarettes.

Collins had been testing Henryk Blonski. In the majority of cases, the missing person turned up eventually, unharmed, but in misper cases where foul play was suspected, the family and closest friends are always the first suspects. Most murders are committed by someone known to the victim.

"Anyway, I can handle him," Collins said.

"If you're sure?"

"Of course, I'm sure. It won't take long. It's not as if I have anything new to tell him. I only spoke to him this morning. I'll tell him I'm checking it out, along with the fifty other things I'm meant to be doing. She's only been missing for a day and a half."

Collins looked at his watch. "Anyway, I'll be back in ten minutes if you still want a lift."

CHAPTER THREE

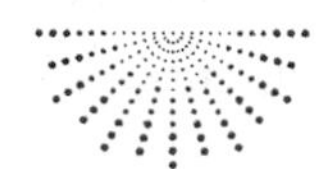

"HOW DID IT GO with Blonski?" Mackinnon asked as they left the back entrance of Wood Street Police Station.

Collins pressed the remote on his key ring, unlocking the car, and shrugged. "He was calmer this afternoon, but he's still really worried."

"Do you think his sister has gone off on her own somewhere?"

"God knows. She's nineteen, so what do you reckon?" Collins sighed. "I think I might be wasting my time looking for her. She probably went out, had a good night, drank a bit too much and right now, she's sleeping off a hangover at a mate's place, lying low because she doesn't want to get nagged by her brother."

Mackinnon nodded. "More than likely."

"So where am I dropping you?" Collins asked as they climbed inside his silver Vauxhall Astra.

"Garfunkels," Mackinnon said.

Collins screwed up his face. "Why are you going there? Bit early for dinner, aren't you?"

"I'm meeting Chloe and her daughters, they've been in London today."

"Ah, school holidays, every parent's nightmare. Still, at least the traffic's lighter."

As Collins drove out of the car park, Mackinnon pulled at his seatbelt, and then started fiddling with the air-conditioning vents.

"What's wrong with you, Jack?" Collins asked, glancing over at Mackinnon before stopping at a set of traffic lights. "You're sweating."

Mackinnon wiped a hand over his forehead. "It's your driving. It makes me nervous."

Collins ignored the dig. "Is this the first time you've met Chloe's daughters?"

Mackinnon nodded.

"Teenagers?"

Mackinnon nodded again.

Collins laughed. "Good luck, mate. You'll need it."

"Cheers, Nick. That boost of confidence was *just* what I needed."

Collins turned to Mackinnon. "You're really worried, aren't you?"

"I'm fine. Just worried I'm never going to get there at this rate. You've gone from driving like a lunatic to pootling along like a granny."

Collins smirked, but he put his foot down.

Mackinnon scowled at the streets and the people they passed. He wished he could wait a little longer before meeting Chloe's daughters. All he really wanted to do now was go back to his flat and have a nice hot shower and a cold beer.

He'd only been seeing Chloe for a couple of months. She was older than him, and he'd known she had kids from the start. He understood why she didn't introduce them to every man she went out with. She said she didn't want to confuse them by introducing them to anyone she wasn't serious about.

Now she'd asked him to meet them.

Mackinnon guessed that meant they were getting serious.

He didn't know which part made him more nervous: getting serious or meeting her kids. Christ, what if they hated him? They probably would. They'd probably resent him for…

"Are you getting out, or what?" Collins asked.

Mackinnon looked out of the passenger window, surprised to see the garish Garfunkels' yellow and red sign in front of him.

"All right. I'm going. See you tomorrow," Mackinnon said, climbing out of the car.

"Have fun." Collins smirked.

Mackinnon waited until Collins pulled away, then stepped through the revolving door onto the red carpet and stood beside a sign asking customers to wait to be seated.

Inside the restaurant, it was still quiet. Mackinnon took a moment and scanned the room, looking for Chloe. There were only one or two occupied tables, both with kids. It was that time of day.

A teenage waitress, with bouncy, black, curly hair wandered over. "Table for one?"

Mackinnon shook his head. "I have a reservation, name of Jack Mackinnon, table for four."

The waitress bent down over the reservation book and put a tick by his name. Then with a cheerful smile, she led him into the restaurant. "We're not very busy at the moment. So you can pick any table."

Mackinnon pointed to a table over in the corner where he could watch the door and asked the waitress for a Coke. When the waitress walked off, he went back over to the entrance and picked up a free copy of the Metro from the rack by the door.

Over the next twenty minutes, Mackinnon flicked through the pages of the Metro and sipped his ice-cold Coke. They were late, which gave him even more time to worry over the idea that both Chloe's daughters were going to hate him on sight.

Five minutes later, he spotted the three of them. They entered the restaurant with their arms entwined like best buddies, giggling as they tried to fit into one section of the revolving door. Mackinnon exhaled a long breath and stood up to greet them.

Chloe's pretty, heart-shaped face lit up when she spotted him. She was dressed in dark blue jeans and a red, fitted top, casual, but still smart. She looked great.

"Jack." Chloe kissed him on the cheek and squeezed his hand. She turned to her daughters. "I'd like you to meet Sarah and Katy."

The two girls stared up at him. They weren't smiling. Not a good sign.

Chloe leaned towards him. "Don't look so worried," she whispered.

The girls didn't look alike. Sarah favoured her mother, fair and slim, almost skinny. Katy, the younger of the two, was dark-haired and at least five inches shorter.

Mackinnon knew both girls had different fathers. Chloe divorced Sarah's father when Sarah was only a baby, but Sarah still saw him on the third Saturday of every month, sometimes more frequently, depending on his work schedule. How much longer that would go on was anyone's guess. He dropped a bombshell last week, telling Chloe he was moving to New Zealand.

Katy's father hadn't wanted anything to do with his daughter. Chloe told Mackinnon they only had a short fling, nothing serious, and Katy's father ditched Chloe shortly after she found out she was pregnant.

Mackinnon smiled at the girls. "Hi, I'm Jack."

Both girls mumbled, "Hello," as they moved toward the table.

Mackinnon pulled out a chair for Chloe. "Did you have a nice day?"

Chloe nodded. "Fantastic. We hit the shops, then went to see the Wicked matinee at the Apollo. I'm thoroughly worn out now, though. I'm starving too." She looked around and waved to get the waitress' attention.

The girls both ordered Cokes, burgers and fries. Chloe asked for the Italian-style chicken and a coffee, and Mackinnon went for the twelve-ounce sirloin steak.

After the drinks arrived. Katy took a sip of Coke, then looked up at Mackinnon. "Mum said you're a policeman."

Mackinnon nodded. "I am."

"Have you seen any dead bodies?"

"Katy!" Chloe shook her head. "That isn't an appropriate question to ask when we are about to eat. Sorry, Jack."

Katy gave Mackinnon a smile that looked more like a grimace. "Sorry."

Sarah looked down at her fizzy drink and used her straw to bash up the ice cubes. Coke sloshed over the sides of the glass.

"Sarah, stop that," Chloe said.

Sarah dropped the straw, slumped back in her seat and stared down at the table.

Chloe, who seemed oblivious to the fact both girls seemed to hate Mackinnon on sight, launched into a detailed description of their day shopping in London.

Mackinnon was glad. He had no idea how to make small talk with two teenage girls who wanted to be here even less than he did.

CHAPTER FOUR

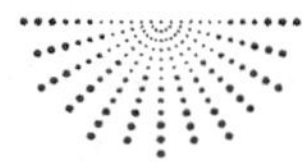

HENRYK BLONSKI WAS STILL reeling from his out-of-control reaction to the detective that morning. He remembered how the detective's shiny suit fabric had felt screwed up in his hands when Henryk had grabbed him. He couldn't understand where the anger had come from. It had risen up inside him, crushed his ribs like a boa constrictor, and set his blood alight.

He felt a flush of mortification when he considered the fact he could be in prison right now, locked up, instead of looking for Anya. What good would he be to his sister then?

Still, on the plus side, maybe he had convinced DC Collins to take Anya's disappearance seriously. If not, then Anya still had Henryk. He would never give up. He would find his sister.

No matter what the police officer said, he knew there

was something wrong. Anya would never make him worry like this.

Henryk called home this morning and spoke to his parents in Poland to check if Anya had been in touch.

As he usually rang home once a week, on Sunday evenings, his mother immediately suspected something was wrong. He didn't want to worry his parents, so he didn't dare tell them Anya was missing. He told them she was fine, working hard and doing well with her dance classes. He said he just wanted to check if she had been in touch because he was working late this week and hadn't seen much of her over the past few days.

Unfortunately, his mother knew him too well. She could tell he was keeping something from her and asked him over and over again to tell her what had happened. He spent twenty minutes trying to convince her that everything was fine, that he just wanted to see if Anya had called home, and made a feeble joke about the phone bill.

He finished the phone call feeling even worse. Anya was missing. Their parents hadn't spoken to her since last week, and now Henryk had made his mother panic. He could tell from her voice she didn't believe him when he said everything was okay. And he knew his mother. She wouldn't let it rest. She would call him again tonight, and he didn't know if he had the energy to make up more lies.

If something had happened to Anya, his parents would want to know immediately. But if she turned up tomorrow, and he had upset them for nothing, Anya would be furious.

Now, Henryk Blonski paused outside a narrow door with peeling, red paint. He raised his hand to knock, then lowered it again. He needed to collect his thoughts first.

As he stood outside Victoria Trent's flat, he tried to plan what he would say. Victoria was a student with Anya at the Star Academy, and Henryk had found her telephone number in Anya's notebook.

When he spoke to Victoria on the phone, she insisted Anya had been offered a great career opportunity, and told him she was sure Anya would be in touch soon.

Of course, Henryk didn't believe it.

Anya had stars in her eyes. She had dreams of being a singer or on the stage. She may have been tricked by a job offer that sounded exotic. She could have been fooled into working as a lap dancer. Or worse...

Anya didn't have many friends in London. There were a few people she knew from her dance classes. She mentioned them now and again, but there was no one Anya was really close to. All of her friends were back in Poland. That was a problem. Henryk couldn't think who Anya might have confided in.

He wasn't convinced that Victoria Trent was a close friend of Anya's, but as he didn't have much else to go on, Henryk wanted to speak to her in person. Maybe Anya told her something, some clue that Henryk could use to find his sister.

Henryk knocked on the door.

The door opened a few centimetres. The safety chain was still on. Two blue eyes, laced with heavy mascara, peered out at him.

Henryk moved closer to the door so she could see him.

"It is Henryk," he said. "Anya's brother."

There was a pause before the door opened to reveal a girl not much older than Anya. She was slim and short, barely five feet tall. Her fair hair was tied back in a messy ponytail, and she wore a loose green top over black leggings. She smelled of violets.

"Victoria?"

The girl nodded.

"Have you heard from her?" Henryk asked, walking into the hall.

Victoria sighed and closed the door behind him.

"No, Henryk," she said, her flip-flops smacking the floor as she walked along the hallway. "I told you. Anya's busy, that's all. She has a new job. She'll be in touch once she's settled."

Henryk gritted his teeth in frustration. She sounded just like that stupid police officer. He wanted to shake some sense into her. Why couldn't anyone else see that Anya must be in danger? Anya would never leave for a new job without telling him.

"What is this job?" Henryk asked. "If it was good, she would have told me. I think it must be bad."

Victoria put her hands on her hips and sighed. "I'm sure Anya's okay, Henryk. Can I get you a drink or something?"

"No." Henryk folded his arms across his chest.

Victoria rolled her eyes. "Well, I need one."

Henryk followed her to the kitchen. Victoria poured a hefty slug of vodka into a pink glass, dropped in two ice cubes and topped it up with Coke, which fizzed over the ice. The foamy bubbles threatened to run over the side of the glass. She picked it up and took an unladylike slurp to avoid the spillage.

"So, tell me about Anya's new job, Victoria."

Victoria took another sip of her drink. "Well." She

paused to think. "I don't know that much about it. But she was going to be an entertainer." Victoria's face brightened. "She said it paid very well."

Henryk scowled. "Entertainer?"

Victoria sighed and leaned back against the door of the chrome-coloured fridge. "I know what you're thinking, Henryk, but really, it's not like that. Anya is a sensible girl. She wouldn't do any of that kind of stuff."

He knew Victoria thought he was being overprotective, acting like an annoying older brother, out to spoil Anya's fun. It wasn't like that. Victoria thought she knew Anya, but she didn't. Not really, not like he did.

His sister would never make him worry like this. If she hadn't been in touch, it must be because something was stopping her.

Or someone, Henryk thought, and a shiver of dread crept along his spine.

"Do you fancy a brownie?" Victoria asked. She pushed forward a pack of four supermarket-brand brownies. The chocolate had melted, smearing the plastic packaging.

"No."

Victoria gazed down at them, then pushed them away. "No. You're right. I shouldn't either."

She left the cakes behind and carried her drink into the front room, and Henryk followed. She perched on the arm of the sofa and crossed her legs, a flip-flop dangling from her foot.

"Don't you want to sit down?" she asked.

"No," Henryk said. "I don't want to sit down. I want to find out what has happened to my sister."

Victoria ran a hand through her blonde hair. "Nothing,

Henryk. Nothing has happened. She probably just needs a bit of space. And I'm not surprised, with you chasing her like this!"

Henryk slumped down into an armchair. He knew he was going about this the wrong way, with the police, as well as Victoria. He needed to get their sympathy, make them understand why he was so worried. Acting like this, he wasn't helping things at all.

Her expression softened, pity shining in her eyes. "I'm sure she'll be in touch soon. Somebody mentioned something about a cruise ship. Perhaps, she had to leave quickly. She'll probably give you a ring as soon as the ship gets to the next port. Just give her a bit of time. She's a big girl. You have to give her space. She's following her dreams, Henryk."

As Victoria raised the glass to her lips, the sleeve of her green top slid a little way down her arm, revealing an angry, red mark. Victoria noticed him looking and yanked the material down to cover it.

Henryk was about to ask how she had hurt herself, then thought better of it. It didn't concern him.

"Did Anya meet a man?" Henryk asked.

Victoria narrowed her eyes. "If she did, it's none of your business. If she wanted to confide in you, she would have."

Henryk got to his feet so quickly, Victoria flinched.

He stepped towards her. "She's my sister, Victoria. Something is wrong. I feel it."

CHAPTER FIVE

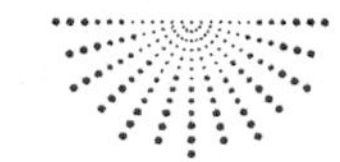

MACKINNON SNUCK A GLANCE at his watch. Where was the food? At least, if he were eating, he wouldn't have to talk.

"Right," Chloe said, standing up. "I'll be back in a minute."

She touched the back of his hand and smiled, then walked off in the direction of the ladies' toilets.

Mackinnon watched her go with a rising sense of panic. Great, now he'd have to talk to the kids on his own.

He turned away from Chloe's retreating back, to find both girls staring at him.

"So," he said. "Sounds like you guys had a great time today."

Mackinnon cringed. Even to his own ears, he sounded like a crummy kid's TV presenter. He sounded false, and kids picked up on that sort of thing. They sensed insincerity, like sharks sense blood. He'd read that somewhere.

Sarah picked up her straw again and started stabbing the ice cubes.

Katy shrugged. "Yeah, it was a nice day."

Mackinnon found himself warming to Katy, if only because she looked as uncomfortable with this meeting as he was.

"So you're a policeman," Sarah said. The way she said policeman made it sound like she thought it was a bad thing.

Mackinnon nodded. "Yes, I am."

"My father's an entrepreneur."

"Really?" Mackinnon said. He had heard all about Sarah's father from Chloe. Lots of names had been mentioned, but entrepreneur was not one of them.

"Yes," Sarah said and waved her straw around, then pointed it at Mackinnon. "Mum said he's quite brilliant. He's invented all kinds of things."

"Nothing that's any good," Katy said and grinned at Mackinnon.

"Oh, my God," Sarah said, turning on her sister. "Take that back!"

"No." Katy smirked.

"You're just jealous because your dad doesn't want anything to do with you!"

"Hey," Mackinnon said.

Surprised at his interruption, both girls stopped arguing and turned to look at him.

"That's not a nice thing to say."

Sarah pulled a face, and Mackinnon felt Katy's brown eyes fixed on him, weighing him up.

He pushed his chair back from the table and took a deep

breath. Please, God, he thought, don't let World War III start while Chloe's in the ladies' toilets. That would not make a good first impression.

When Mackinnon saw Chloe walking back towards the table, he sighed with relief.

"Mum, Katy's saying nasty things about my dad," Sarah said the moment Chloe pulled out her chair and sat down.

Chloe pursed her lips and looked disappointed, probably just as disappointed in Mackinnon as she was in the girls.

He knew he should say something to clear the air; but he had no idea what.

Chloe sat down, shook out her napkin, and placed it on her lap.

The waitress arrived with the first two plates of food. She set down Mackinnon's steak and chips.

"Can I get you guys any sauces? Any more drinks?" the waitress asked.

When no one else replied, Mackinnon shook his head and said, "No, thanks, we're fine."

They ate their meals in miserable silence.

Mackinnon cut into his steak and took a large bite. The evening wasn't a complete failure. The steak was pretty good.

* * *

Henryk Blonski's mind was whirring when he left Victoria Trent's flat. Victoria didn't realise it, but she had given him an idea.

Victoria was a nice enough girl, but she didn't know

where Anya was any more than he did. That didn't matter. He was still glad he had spoken to her because their conversation triggered a memory.

Now Henryk was sure he had the information he needed to find his sister. One phone call would be enough to confirm his suspicions. His stomach churned with nerves.

As soon as he left Victoria's flat and began walking toward the stairwell, Henryk reached for the mobile in his pocket. Then he stopped abruptly and looked behind him into the empty corridor.

He shivered.

There was no one there, but he had the uncanny sensation of being watched, like an antelope stalked by a predator on one of those TV wildlife documentaries.

Henryk loosened the grip on his phone and left it in his pocket. He wouldn't make the call in here. Outside would be safer. He didn't want to risk being overheard by anyone who might be lingering in the flats.

Outside in the cool night air, Henryk strode across the square and climbed over the three-foot tall, spiky, black railings that cordoned off the grass. He stood under the rustling branches of a beech tree and leaned back on its smooth bark. He took out his phone and dialled another number that had been in Anya's notebook.

When the man answered, Henryk shouted at him down the phone. He told him he knew what had happened to Anya. To his surprise, the man didn't deny it.

Instead, he laughed, a cold, grating laugh that chilled Henryk to the bone.

Henryk started to beg and plead for his sister. If only he

would release her, give Anya back to him, Henryk promised to tell no one. The man on the other end hung up and Henryk was left listening to the cold, dull sound of silence.

It was enough evidence for Henryk. Now he knew who had Anya. He was sure of it.

His limbs trembled. He wiped his hands, slick with sweat, on his jeans. He'd known there was something wrong. He'd felt it. But this? He had never expected this. He stared with hatred at the phone in his hand and wanted to smash it.

He raised his palms and clamped them against his ears. He could still hear the man's cruel laughter in his mind.

Hundreds of ideas crowded Henryk's mind at once. What could he do? Go to the police? They weren't interested before, would they even believe him now?

No. The police would take too long. Henryk didn't have time to waste. He had to act now.

Maybe he could ask a friend to help? But who did he know in England that he could trust with something so important? Henryk took a deep breath.

No one.

He would have to do it alone.

He wasn't afraid. He just needed to be prepared. That evil man would regret the day he ever even looked at Anya. Henryk would make sure of it.

He looked up and saw the light on in Victoria's flat. She was peeking through the frothy, net curtains. She lifted her hand. Henryk waved back, then turned away, jumped over the railings and strode across the green.

He walked fast, slightly out of breath. He had to get

back to his flat. He couldn't confront this man unarmed. That would be madness.

Henryk stuffed his hands into the pockets of his jeans and hunched his shoulders as he turned onto the main road, completely unaware that he was being followed.

CHAPTER SIX

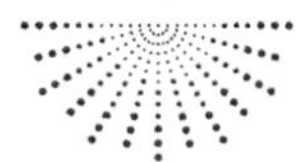

MACKINNON GOT BACK TO his Docklands studio flat at just after seven pm. He opened the front door, tapped his code into the alarm and leaned down to pick up the post.

He elbowed the door closed behind him, put the mail on the kitchen counter and walked straight to the fridge and pulled out a bottle of Tiger beer.

What an evening.

He moved across to the bar and picked up a bottle opener, frowning as he hooked it over the cap. The bar was one of the few pieces of furniture he owned. Bottles of spirits were lined up along the polished wooden top. Mackinnon's studio flat was perfect for a single bloke.

Mackinnon took a couple of gulps of beer and headed over to the bedroom area. Within seconds, he'd stripped off his work suit and pulled on jeans and an old, comfortable t-shirt. He picked up his beer and wandered back into the open plan living area, remembering how Chloe's girls had stared at him tonight, weighing him up, judging him. He had a feeling he came up short.

He looked around his compact flat. If things did get serious with Chloe, he could say goodbye to this kind of lifestyle.

Chloe was just past forty with two kids already, so if things worked out with her, chances were he'd never have kids of his own.

He took another mouthful of beer and stood beside the floor-to-ceiling window, looking out at the London skyline.

Why was he thinking like this? It wasn't like him. Trying to plan things out in advance, worrying about the details. Maybe because if it didn't work out, it would affect more than just the two of them. Maybe because he really did want things to work out this time.

He should just play it by ear, see how things went. No point worrying about what might happen.

He took another sip of beer.

He loved this view. The flat was sold to him with views of the Thames. Not true. Not unless you counted the glimpse from the bathroom. You could see a sliver of water if you stood on the toilet seat and stuck your head out the window.

Despite that, it was still a great outlook. The London skyline, he loved it. The mix of old and new. He never tired of looking at it.

Mackinnon's great-grandfather had worked as a stevedore at the docks, near to where Mackinnon's block of flats now stood. Things had changed drastically since then. The city rumbled along, constantly changing, consuming and evolving.

One Canada Square, the largest tower in Canary Wharf, dominated the skyline, blinking against the dark blue sky. Lights were on in the offices, either businessmen and women working late, or maybe cleaners. London never stopped.

It was hard to believe the bombings happened just last year. London carried on... It always did, swallowing tragedies, producing new generations with new visions of what the city meant to them.

Mackinnon walked away from the window, picked up the TV remote and flopped down on the sofa.

Reality shows of one sort or another were on the first few channels he flicked through. One was a singing competition, another a fly-on-the-wall documentary about a set of teenage girls trying to make it in the modelling industry.

Not much on TV then. He considered heading to the gym. There was one in his apartment building for the residents. Even though it was so close, he still found reasons not to go, such as another beer in the fridge calling his name. That was the trouble with Tiger beer, he thought, walking to the kitchen then throwing the empty bottle in the recycling box: the bottles were just too small.

The phone rang. Mackinnon put the TV on mute and reached for his mobile. It was Chloe.

"Hey, you," she said. "We just got home. The girls are worn out, too tired to even argue."

Mackinnon glanced at the silent TV screen, where a young girl was sobbing her heart out because a panel of self-appointed experts had crushed her dreams.

"Good journey?" he asked.

"Yes. The train was busy, but we managed to get seats, so it wasn't too bad. Listen, Jack, I have an idea."

"Yeah?"

"Tomorrow night, the girls won't be around. Why don't you come up and stay the night?"

"In Oxford?"

"Yes. I'll make dinner. It'll be nice to spend some more time together, won't it?"

Mackinnon paused for a moment. He was on earlies, so he'd have to get up at the crack of dawn to get back to London the next day for work, but what the hell. It would be worth it. "Sounds good. Shall I aim to get there around six?"

"Perfect."

After Mackinnon hung up, he walked across to the TV. A middle-aged woman in a tiny, tight leather skirt and scarlet corset, caked in makeup filled the screen with her mouth open as if she were screaming. Mackinnon was glad the sound was down. He reached over and switched off the power button.

Everyone was hungry for their fifteen minutes of fame. It was almost an obsession in Britain these days. He didn't understand it.

CHAPTER SEVEN

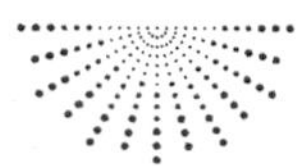

HENRYK BLONSKI'S HAND SHOOK as he pulled his keys from the back pocket of his jeans. Adrenaline flooded his system. He stood close to his front door and fumbled with the brass key. Why wouldn't the stupid thing fit in the lock?

His mother's voice filled his mind: *"Spiesz sie powoli."* More haste, less speed.

He forced himself to slow down and deliberately and carefully inserted the key into the lock.

He would make him pay, this evil man who had Anya.

Henryk's mind filled with images of revenge. He had a knife in his flat. It wasn't as good as a gun, but there was no time to organise something like that.

He needed to get the knife then he would...

Henryk turned. He thought he heard a noise. Maybe footsteps?

There was nothing but the sound of his own raspy

breathing and pounding heart beat. Henryk turned back to the front door and pushed it open. He needed to hurry and get the knife. He would make the man realise he picked on the wrong family.

He must have singled out poor Anya because she seemed like a sweet Polish girl, far from her family and friends. Well, he would soon realise Anya had someone. She had him.

As he started to push the door open, he hesitated. Perhaps he should go to the police. Perhaps he shouldn't take the knife with him. He didn't want to hurt anyone.

Henryk shook his head. It would be madness to go unarmed. Henryk had to prove he meant business, and if someone got hurt…

Cel uswieca srodki. The end justifies the means.

He was so consumed by his thoughts, he didn't hear the heavy footsteps closing in behind him.

He didn't turn until the first sickening thud reverberated in his skull.

Senses dulled, Henryk raised a hand to his head. A pathetic gesture of self-defence. What good were his hands against a hammer?

Henryk staggered. Dazed, he lifted his head to face his attacker.

"You…"

Blood dripped in his eyes. He couldn't see.

The second blow was swift, vicious and final.

Henryk fell to the floor and felt the warm, sticky, wetness spread over his scalp, leaking down over his face and neck.

His attacker was talking, saying something, but the voice was fading.

As Henryk Blonski's life slipped away, his final thought echoed in his mind. Simple and full of regret: I'm sorry, Anya.

CHAPTER EIGHT

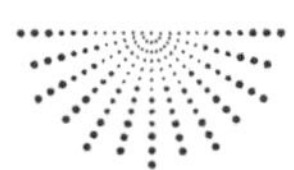

THE FOLLOWING MORNING, COLLINS called as Mackinnon was standing by the kitchen counter, eating a slice of toast and marmalade and polishing off his first cup of coffee.

"I'll be passing yours in five minutes if you want a lift," Collins said.

Collins drove into work every day from Essex. Mackinnon didn't envy him that journey. But to be fair, a policeman's salary went a lot further in Romford. Collins couldn't fit himself, his wife and two kids into a flat the size of Mackinnon's.

Mackinnon usually caught the DLR, from South Quay, but he wouldn't pass up the opportunity of a more comfortable journey. He told Collins he would be waiting downstairs in five minutes, then hung up.

He patted himself down, mentally checking off his morning list. Wallet, mobile, keys… He picked up his coat and headed out the door, yawning. He hated the early shift.

Well, he hated the early shift in the mornings, but loved it in the afternoons.

As Mackinnon climbed in the passenger seat of Collins' silver Astra, with a cheery "Hello," Collins shifted in his seat, looking guilty.

"What is it?" Mackinnon asked.

Collins pulled away from the curb. "I have an ulterior motive for giving you a lift."

Mackinnon frowned. "And I thought you offered because you couldn't get enough of my sparkling personality. Go on then, what is it?"

"I want to get your opinion on Henryk Blonski."

"The guy whose sister's missing?"

Collins nodded as he pulled out into the heavy traffic. "I couldn't sleep last night. I kept thinking about it."

"You said it yourself, people go missing all the time. Usually, by choice."

"Yeah, I know. There's just something odd about it. I mean, it doesn't look suspicious on the surface. The most likely scenario is that she went off on her own. But, I don't know, something just doesn't feel right."

Collins sighed, his eyes fixed on the road ahead. "Maybe the brother's paranoia is rubbing off on me, but I'd appreciate your take on it."

"Sure." Mackinnon looked at the digital clock on the dashboard and tried to tune out the irritatingly cheerful voice coming from the radio. "We're a bit early for a house call, aren't we?"

It was just before seven am.

"I don't think he'll mind. I think he'll be grateful to know we are looking into his sister's disappearance. Yesterday, he was mouthing off about me not taking her disappearance seriously enough."

They made it through the morning traffic in surprisingly good time and pulled up outside the red-brick council flats of Jubilee House on the Towers Estate.

Most property in the City of London was occupied by businesses, and residential areas were relatively rare.

The unimaginatively named Towers Estate was a collection of tower blocks. The area had been gradually extended over time, so there was no uniformity, just a mishmash of buildings. Low-rise, red-brick blocks mixed with grey, high-rise towers, and between the buildings, a network of dark alleyways crisscrossed the estate. The alleyways weren't the kind of place any law-abiding person would choose to walk alone at night.

The Towers Estate had the largest residential population in the City of London, and it caused the police a great deal of trouble.

A couple of kids, of senior-school age, leaned against an old, black BMW three series, trying to stare Mackinnon and Collins down. They wore school uniforms, shirts untucked, ties in their pockets. It was anyone's guess if they would actually make it to school.

Mackinnon glanced at his watch. Seven twenty am. At least they were up early. Their eyes followed Mackinnon and Collins. They may not have guessed they were police, but they knew Mackinnon and Collins didn't belong in the neighbourhood.

"Over here. It's number sixty-two, Jubilee House,"

Collins said, heading to the second entrance to the block of flats.

Jubilee House was a typical sixties building and relatively low-rise compared to other flats in the area, at only seven storeys tall.

The blue doors were tagged and spray-painted with graffiti.

Despite the early hour, the sun was already warm. It was going to be another hot one. Mackinnon caught a whiff of the rotten stench from the bins, already cooking in the warm weather, as he passed the base of the rubbish chute. He held his breath until he reached the security doors.

Someone had propped open the door with half a breeze block. Despite the bright, early morning light outside, the entrance was dark. The fluorescent strip light above the entrance was broken. A crack ran straight across the plastic casing. A strange, ominous sensation crept over Mackinnon. He didn't want to go in.

Mackinnon shook the feeling off and stepped inside.

* * *

The inside of Jubilee House wasn't much better than the outside. The lobby was ingrained with dirt. The floor was swept clean, but grime, driven into the tiles over the years, wasn't that easy to remove, and a quick once-over with a broom wasn't going to get rid of it.

The hallway smelled of fried food, spices and bacon.

Mackinnon looked at Collins. "Stairs?"

Collins nodded. "Definitely."

Mackinnon always avoided the lifts on the Towers

Estate. They always smelt awful, and six floors was a long time to hold your breath.

They took the stairs two at a time.

There were only two flats on each floor. There was no central stairwell and the staircase led straight onto the lobby. So they had to walk past the flats on each floor to get to the next set of stairs.

As they passed the first floor flats, Mackinnon caught a whiff of urine, mixed with the smell of bleach, where some poor resident had tried to clean it up.

They increased their speed, and by the time they had reached the second floor, Collins was wheezing.

"You need to get a bit more exercise, Nick," Mackinnon said, grinning.

"I'm perfectly fit, thank you very much." And to prove his point, Collins climbed the stairs faster, moving ahead of Mackinnon.

"And I'll have you know, Debra likes my physique."

"She likes the soft, cuddly type, then?"

Collins turned to face Mackinnon, swore, then climbed more quickly.

Mackinnon felt his own breath coming faster by the time they reached the fifth floor, not that he would admit it to anyone, especially not Collins.

Between gasps for air, Collins managed to say, "I thought I'd tell Henryk Blonski we would keep his sister's details on record, but unless he can give us some more information, there's not a lot… Shit."

Mackinnon reached the top of the stairs behind Collins and almost bumped into him.

"What?"

He looked over Collins' shoulder and saw the gruesome sight of Henryk Blonski, or what was left of him.

Henryk Blonski lay outside the door of his flat, his body curled up, and his mouth open in a silent scream.

For a moment, both Mackinnon and Collins stared down at him. Then Mackinnon crouched down a couple of feet away from the body. He didn't want to move closer and risk contaminating the scene.

His eyes took in his surroundings, looking for details, something that might explain what had happened and why.

Beside him, Collins let out a shaky breath.

"I'll call it in," Collins said as he moved past Mackinnon to walk back down the stairs.

Mackinnon watched him go, then turned his attention back to Henryk Blonski. He stared at the wound on the back of Blonski's head. Some of the blood had dried and darkened, matting his hair and staining his clothes. His body had been here for a while, hours at least.

He could smell the blood, taste the metallic tang of it. But that had to be his imagination. The horror of the scene was influencing his perception. He needed to focus.

Mackinnon forced himself to look away from the body and take in the scene. It looked as though Henryk Blonski had been killed by repeated blows to the back of his head. But there was nothing in the immediate vicinity that could have been the murder weapon.

Could he have been attacked elsewhere then staggered back home, only to die on his doorstep? Mackinnon found it hard to believe he could have walked anywhere with that gaping hole in the back of his head. And the only blood was around the body, right by Henryk Blonski's front door.

There was no blood trail, which suggested Henryk Blonski had been attacked outside his home. But why?

It was a rough area, stabbings were not uncommon, but this had been a furious attack. How someone could inflict this sort of damage on another person, spoke of rage, hatred. It seemed personal.

A mugging? But if it were a mugging, why hit him so many times? Did he fight back?

Or was this something to do with Blonski's sister's disappearance?

Directly opposite Henryk Blonski's body was the door to the second flat on this floor. There were a total of fourteen flats on this side of Jubilee House. Someone must have heard something. The Towers Estate was rough, but even here, surely a man couldn't be bludgeoned to death without anyone noticing.

CHAPTER NINE

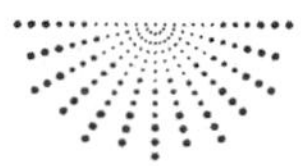

BLUE-SUITED CSIS WERE already filing through the entrance of Jubilee House when DI Green arrived on the scene.

Five-foot-eight, with a shock of prematurely white hair and startling blue eyes that never seemed to miss a thing, DI Green radiated authority. He stood with the early morning sun behind him.

Mackinnon squinted at the detective inspector, the sun's glare hurting his eyes. He felt pressure at the base of his skull, the beginnings of a headache.

"Tell me what we've got."

DI Green spoke to Mackinnon, but Collins answered, telling the DI how they found Henryk Blonski's body.

Hierarchy in the police force could be a tricky issue. Technically, as Mackinnon was a detective sergeant and Collins was still a detective constable, Mackinnon outranked him, but Mackinnon had known Collins for years, and they had a good working relationship.

Mackinnon would never insist on Collins calling him sir. Some higher-ranking officers did, as they thought it showed respect for the chain of command. Mackinnon would rather be on first name terms with someone he trusted. DI Green, on the other hand, was an officer who liked the boundaries clearly marked. He was called DI Green or sir. There was no first-name familiarity with him.

Mackinnon listened as Collins filled DI Green in.

He knew Collins needed to handle this one, to talk it through and explain his actions. Immediately after they found Henryk Blonski's body, Mackinnon asked if Collins was all right. Collins said he was fine and brushed off Mackinnon's concern, but he was clearly badly shaken.

It wasn't only the horror of finding Henryk Blonski on the floor of Jubilee House with his head caved in, though God knows that was bad enough. It was because Collins kept asking himself if he should have acted differently and whether he could have prevented Blonski's death.

Of course, it wasn't Collins' fault, but pointing that out right now wouldn't be helpful. So Mackinnon kept quiet.

While Collins talked, DI Green pulled his incident bag from the boot of his car. They walked towards the blue and white tape pulled across the entrance to the flats. A young PC standing guard recorded their names in the log and stepped back, letting them enter.

Mackinnon watched them walk inside the taped path marking the route to Henryk Blonski's body. Mackinnon didn't follow. There were enough people in there already –

crime scene photographers and scenes of crime officers collecting evidence.

Instead, Mackinnon took in the view outside Jubilee House and fumbled in his pocket for an antacid tablet. He always seemed to have indigestion these days.

The kids and the black BMW were long gone. In their place, other residents had gathered to try and work out what had happened. They watched the police suspiciously. Every now and then, one of them would approach the flustered PC guarding the entrance and demand to know what was going on.

A few minutes later, DI Green came stalking out of Jubilee House, followed by Collins and the crime scene manager.

DI Green looked up at Mackinnon. "Brutal. Poor bastard."

Mackinnon nodded.

"Looks like he was hit from behind," Collins said. "He didn't stand a chance."

Collins' face was grey as he looked down at his shiny, black shoes. Mackinnon made up his mind to talk to him again later and make sure he really was all right.

"Briefing," DI Green said, turning and walking back to his car. "Wood Street in one hour."

"Do you know what happened?" a woman with a toddler balanced on her hip asked Mackinnon and Collins. The kid had a runny nose and rubbed at it with the back of one hand, managing to wipe it all over his face.

"Do you live near here?" Mackinnon asked.

"Yeah, I live in there, don't I?" The woman nodded at the PC standing by the blue and white tape, guarding the entrance to Jubilee House. "But he won't let me back in."

She had a shiny, red face and wore a short, denim skirt and a white vest with a black bra underneath. One of her bra straps had slipped down over her right shoulder.

"We will be as quick as we can," Collins said. "But a man has been…"

"Well, that's nothing to do with me, is it?" She yanked up her elastic bra strap and snapped it back into place. "I need to get inside and get my little boy's milk. It's too hot to stand around out here."

"Did you notice anything unusual last night?" Collins asked.

"What?"

"Did you see anyone hanging around?" Collins asked. "What number do you live at?"

Mackinnon watched the shutters come down. Her face blank, she narrowed her eyes.

"Why are you asking me questions? I haven't done anything wrong. I'm just minding my own business." She tucked a strand of greasy hair behind her ear.

"Just tell us what number you live at," Collins snapped.

Mackinnon raised his eyebrows at Collins' tone.

"All right. Calm down." She lifted the kid onto her other hip. "Number sixty."

Mackinnon paused for a minute, trying to remember the layouts of the flats. "Then you live opposite Mr. Blonski at number sixty-two."

"The Polish fella? Yeah."

"When did you last see him?"

"Oh, I can't remember. He keeps to himself. Lives with a girl. Snooty cow, if you ask me. Always looking down her nose at everyone. She asked me once if I wanted to use their washing machine. She thought my washing machine was broken because Taylor's clothes were dirty. I mean, the cheek of it. Kids get dirty, I told her. That's just what they do."

"What's your name?"

"Tina Mathews."

"Were you at home last night?"

"No." Her eyes narrowed again. "I was at my boyfriend's place."

Collins pulled out his notepad and took down her boyfriend's address, while Mackinnon spoke to a couple of uniforms and asked them to start canvassing the other flats. Someone must have seen something.

When Collins finished talking to Tina Mathews, he looked at his watch and waved Mackinnon over.

"The crime scene manager said we can take a look at the flat now if you think we have time before the DI's briefing?"

Mackinnon nodded. "Time for a quick look."

Mackinnon and Collins made their way back to Henryk Blonski's apartment, keeping to the path marked out by tape. "What do you reckon, Jack?" Collins asked. "Is it a coincidence that his sister is missing?"

"Could be, but I don't think so."

Collins was quiet for a while as they walked up the stairs, then he turned to Mackinnon and said, "Doc said he was killed with a blunt object, a blow to the back of the head. Two or three blows, perhaps."

They reached the sixth floor, and they both looked down at the dark bloodstains on the yellow tiles.

The photographs had been taken and evidence collected. The clean-up crew would arrive soon to wash the blood from the public areas.

Mackinnon and Collins stepped over Henryk Blonski's blood and into the flat.

The paint on the walls was old and slightly yellowing. The flat clearly hadn't been decorated for some time. The carpet, worn thin along the centre, was a dirty green colour.

Despite the fact the walls were crying out for fresh paint, and the carpet should have been replaced years ago, Mackinnon's first impression was that the flat was clean. He had been inside many homes on the Towers Estate, and this was easily the cleanest he'd seen. The smell of furniture polish lingered in the air.

The flat had an empty feeling to it already.

They walked into the living room. There were a couple of cheap armchairs, upholstered in an ugly, green fabric. A small table and chairs set back against one wall. A small TV set, no stereo. The carpet, like the one in the hall, had seen better days, but it was clean.

On the mantelpiece, above an ancient-looking gas fire, there was a row of framed photos. Mackinnon picked one up and took a closer look.

"Anya and Henryk?"

Collins walked over and peered at the photograph. "Yes. Henryk gave me a couple of photos of Anya yesterday. Pretty, isn't she?"

"So young. Nineteen, did you say?"

"Yeah. She looked a bit older in the photos Henryk gave me, so I think this is an older one."

Mackinnon stared at their smiling faces. What could have happened? Henryk Blonski was now dead. Was Anya dead, too? Mackinnon found it hard to reconcile this image of Henryk Blonski, with the battered body he saw this morning. The Henryk Blonski in the photograph was handsome, confident and radiated vitality. He looked so full of life.

Mackinnon replaced the photo next to the ticking carriage clock on the mantelpiece and glanced over at Collins, who seemed to be staring at a spot on the floor. "Are you okay?"

Collins shook his head. "Oh, yeah, fine."

"You look pale. Maybe you should get some air."

Collins blew out a long breath, puffing out his cheeks. "It's just... You never get used to it, do you? The poor bloke. He seemed like a nice enough..." Collins took another deep breath before walking out of the room, shaking his head.

Mackinnon picked up the photograph again, this time focusing on Anya's face.

"What happened to you?" he muttered.

Anya Blonski had wide-spaced, blue eyes and her smile revealed a gap between her front teeth. Innocent. That was the word that came first into Mackinnon's thoughts as he stared at her. He put the photograph back on the mantelpiece.

Appearances could be deceptive.

Mackinnon entered Anya's bedroom next. He stopped by the door and took in the scene. Like the rest of the flat, her bedroom was very tidy. Sequinned scatter cushions and turquoise throws covered the bed and the small chair next to it. A fluffy rug lay next to the bed. She had tried to make the place homely, to put her stamp on it.

In the corner of the room was a narrow, pine wardrobe, with a few marks and dents in the door. Mackinnon opened it. It was packed full of colourful dresses, jeans and shoes. He felt a tug of disappointment and frowned. This wasn't good. If she *had* gone off somewhere, she would have taken her clothes with her.

But maybe she did. Maybe she had lots of clothes and only took her favourite things with her.

He could hear Collins moving about next door in Henryk's bedroom.

Mackinnon looked at his watch. They would have to make a move soon to get back in time for the briefing. He looked in on Collins. "Find anything?"

Collins held up a slim, black notebook. "Address book. It's all in Polish. We can get a Polish interpreter in to take a look. Should help us contact his next of kin anyway."

"Did they have more family over here?"

Collins shook his head. "Henryk said it was just him and Anya. He said he called his parents back in Poland in case they heard from Anya, but he didn't tell them she was missing. He didn't want to make them worry." Collins sighed and slipped the notebook in a plastic bag, then peeled off his gloves. "I don't suppose he imagined how this would turn out."

"There's no sign of a disturbance inside the flat," Mackinnon said.

"No," Collins said. "It looks like whoever attacked him

caught him outside. Maybe they waited for him to leave, or to come home."

"So tell me again about Anya's disappearance," Mackinnon said.

"Anya Blonski, nineteen, Polish. Hasn't been seen for two days. No criminal record. No boyfriend. Very few friends, according to her brother, and she didn't socialise much. She worked at Starbucks part-time, attended a school of some sort the rest of the time, taking dance classes."

From the way the details rolled off his tongue, Mackinnon knew the facts must have been going around and around in Collins' head as he tried to make sense of it all, looking for something he might have missed.

Collins and Mackinnon got back to Wood Street Station in time for the briefing. Mackinnon was expecting DI Green to hand the Blonski case to MIT, the Major Investigation Team, leaving Mackinnon and Collins to go back and finish up their paperwork on a case involving a Romanian gang of thieves targeting tourists in the city.

To Mackinnon's surprise, DI Green outlined their preliminary strategy on the Blonski case and began to allocate tasks to Collins and him. He explained MIT were closing in on a suspect, a taxi driver who cruised the city, picking up young men outside clubs, then sexually assaulting them.

"It's all hands on deck in MIT at the moment," DI Green said. "Officially, MIT are handling the Blonski case, but for now, you two will need to do most of the leg work."

The rest of Mackinnon's day was spent with a phone clamped to his ear, tracking down acquaintances of Henry and Anya Blonski in the UK and Poland.

CHAPTER TEN

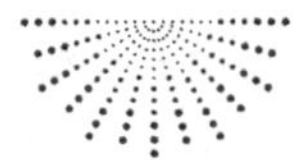

CHLOE LIVED WITH HER daughters in a three-bedroom semi in Oxford. As Mackinnon drove down the Woodstock Road in the Mondeo he borrowed from a friend, he lowered the volume on the radio and looked out for Chloe's house. He'd only visited once before, and that had been in daylight.

Mackinnon looked at the clock on the dashboard. Nine pm. He hoped Chloe was the understanding type.

Finally spotting the sign for Cavendish Place on his right, Mackinnon turned in and nosed the car into the gravel drive of number seventy. Chloe opened the front door before he'd even gotten out of the car.

As his feet crunched over the gravel, he smelled freshly cut grass and the smoky tang of a bonfire. It was a refreshing smell, so different from London.

Chloe grinned at him. "I thought you might have gotten lost."

Mackinnon leaned forward to kiss her cheek. "Sorry, it's been a hell of a day at work."

Chloe frowned. "I don't suppose you're allowed to tell me about it?"

"I don't think you'd really want to hear about it," Mackinnon said, and truthfully, he didn't want to talk about it. He wanted to switch off for the evening, to enjoy Chloe's company, and forget work. Most of all, he wanted to wipe away the image of the bloody, battered Henryk Blonski, which seemed to be indelibly printed in his mind.

They walked through to the kitchen, and Mackinnon shrugged off his jacket as Chloe poured him a glass of Shiraz.

"Are you hungry? I thought I'd make pasta."

"Sounds great." Mackinnon took the glass of red wine Chloe held out to him. "Do you need me to do anything?"

"No, there's not much to do." She started to chop up some chorizo. "You can put some music on if you like."

Mackinnon wandered over to the iPod speaker station and started scrolling through the tracks. "Anything in particular you fancy listening to?" Mackinnon asked, noticing she had a lot of classical music stored in the iPod.

Chloe filled a saucepan with water and set it on the hob to boil. "You choose."

Mackinnon picked out an oldie. "Sam Cooke's Greatest Hits." Chloe turned and smiled at Mackinnon as Sam began to croon, *"You send me."*

A pile of magazines sat on the shelf beside the speakers. Mackinnon glanced at one with a teenage girl on the cover. She was plastered in makeup and held a banner declaring her the winner of a singing competition.

Chloe noticed him looking. "They're Sarah's magazines. You can move them if they're in the way."

Mackinnon shook his head. "They're not."

"They are weekly instalments of the latest Singstar competition. Sarah has every copy. They are a bloody rip-off, four pounds a copy."

"Reality shows seem to be on all the time these days," Mackinnon said. He watched Chloe pour a dash of olive oil into a pan followed by the chorizo, a few chopped cherry tomatoes and a handful of basil.

"Yeah, both girls are mad about them."

The pasta sauce bubbled away in the pan. It looked simple enough, but the delicious aroma made Mackinnon's stomach rumble.

"That smells delicious."

Chloe picked up her wine glass and looked at Mackinnon over the rim. "Well, they do say the way to a man's heart is through his stomach."

Mackinnon grinned. "Where are the girls tonight?"

"Sarah's spending the night at her father's and Katy is staying at a friend's for a sleepover."

"How's Sarah taking the New Zealand thing? Has her father told her he's going yet?"

Chloe nodded. "Yes. She's taking it surprisingly well. She's full of chatter about how her father told her she could stay with him for the holidays, and maybe even attend university out there. In fact, she doesn't seem angry with him at all."

"That's good," Mackinnon said and took a sip of his wine.

"Yes, her dad's flavour of the month. But I can't do anything right at the moment. I tried to explain that Stuart would need time to settle and flights to New Zealand are expensive, so maybe she shouldn't expect too much. She accused me of trying to ruin her relationship with him." Chloe shrugged. "It's difficult. I don't want to be the one who pours cold water all over her dreams, but I don't want her to be disappointed. I know he's going to let her down again."

Chloe looked up. "Sorry. I shouldn't be boring you with all this. It's your fault. You're just too easy to talk to." She spooned a serving of pasta into a large white bowl and handed it to Mackinnon. "Let's talk about less depressing things!"

After finishing a second helping of pasta, Mackinnon sat back on Chloe's sofa, feeling happily stuffed and yawned. "Sorry. It's been a long day."

"You must be shattered you were on earlies today, weren't you?"

Mackinnon nodded, doing his best to stifle another yawn.

"Maybe you need an early night." Chloe raised an eyebrow suggestively.

Suddenly Mackinnon felt wide-awake. "Now, there's an offer I can't refuse."

* * *

Upstairs, clothes off, under the covers, Chloe suddenly sat bolt upright. "What was that?"

"What?" Mackinnon said, sitting up next to her.

Then Mackinnon heard it too. A low rattle, then the sound of someone moving about.

"There's someone downstairs." Chloe gripped his arm.

"It's probably one of the girls."

"No," Chloe said. "They would have phoned to tell me if they were coming home."

Mackinnon swung his legs over the bed and put on his jeans. "I'll check it out."

He padded out of the bedroom, barefoot and bare-chested, and paused to listen. He could hear a definite rustling.

There *was* someone down there.

The noise was coming from the kitchen. He walked down the stairs as quietly as he could. His foot pressed on a creaky step, and he winced, holding his breath.

The rustling continued. Whoever was down there hadn't heard him. He descended the rest of the stairs as quickly as possible and crept down the hallway. It was dark, and he was in an unfamiliar house, but he didn't want to switch the lights on and warn the intruder he was coming.

He walked along the dark hallway, trailing a hand along the wall to guide him. There was a small table with the telephone on it around here somewhere, wasn't there?

Mackinnon's toes found the table before his eyes did. He clenched his teeth and swallowed the swear words he wanted to shout.

The kitchen door was partially open, and he pulled it open a fraction further, so he could see what he was up against. There was no point barrelling in if the intruder had a weapon. Mackinnon didn't have much of a plan, but it made sense to take a look at what he was up against.

A crash sounded in the kitchen.

Mackinnon would never admit it to anyone else, but it felt as if his heart missed a couple of beats. He wiped his clammy hands on his jeans and inched forwards closer to the door.

The door swung open and connected with Mackinnon's face.

He let rip the swear words he'd swallowed only a moment earlier.

Christ, that hurt. He staggered back, nose burning, eyes watering.

He saw a silhouetted figure shift in front of him. Furious, he shot forward, arms outstretched. Whoever just broke his nose was going to pay.

Then Mackinnon heard a scream. A woman's voice. Chloe?

Mackinnon turned, confused; then light flooded the hallway.

In front of him stood Sarah, Chloe's elder daughter, her mouth open, ready to scream again.

Chloe's pale face appeared over the banister.

"Jack?" she called. "You scared me. I thought... Oh, Sarah. What are you doing home?"

Sarah's lower lip trembled. "What's *he* doing here?"

Chloe tied the cord on her dressing gown, folded her arms across her chest and walked down the rest of the stairs.

"Jack is staying here tonight," she said. "Now answer my question, young lady. What are you doing home? You're supposed to be staying at your father's."

Then Chloe noticed Mackinnon's bloody nose for the first time and gasped. "Did you do that, Sarah?"

"Not on purpose!"

"It was the door," Mackinnon muttered, tenderly touching his nose to see if it was broken. But he may as well not have bothered for all the attention Chloe and Sarah paid him.

Sarah glared at her mother. She no longer looked scared. She looked furious. "Oh, I see. Now Jack's around, I can't even come home when I want to. You want me out of the way, is that it?"

Sarah pushed past Mackinnon and Chloe as she stomped upstairs.

"Honestly, that girl!" Chloe looked up at him. "Oh dear, I think we'd better get some ice on that, Jack."

Mackinnon followed her into the kitchen, and Chloe pulled some ice cubes out of the freezer.

"Sarah seemed pretty upset," Mackinnon said. "Do you want me to leave?"

Chloe shook her head. "No. Sarah will come round. It's not as if I'm bringing home a different man every night."

"I should hope not," Mackinnon said.

Chloe smiled. "The girls will have to get used to you being around."

Mackinnon touched the side of his nose, tentatively.

"I'm so sorry, Jack. I really didn't think the girls would be coming home. Does it hurt?"

"Yes." Mackinnon snatched up the ice, held it to his face, then opened the fridge and pulled out a bottle of beer. He jerked open the top and took a long gulp.

Chloe moved towards him and put her hand on his shoulder.

Mackinnon decided to let her off. It wasn't really her fault he felt like a complete idiot.

"It's stopped bleeding now anyway," he said generously.

"It wasn't quite the romantic evening I had planned," Chloe said. "I really am sorry."

Mackinnon took another mouthful of beer. "You're not getting off that easily. You'll have to make it up to me," he said with a lopsided grin.

"And how will I do that?" Chloe asked.

Mackinnon put his arm around Chloe's shoulders, pulling her close. "If we put our heads together, I'm sure we can come up with something."

CHAPTER ELEVEN

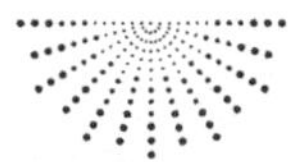

ON FRIDAY MORNING, IN her blue and white, tiny bathroom, Victoria Trent looked down and gasped in horror.

No way. That could not be right. She refused to believe it.

She jumped off the scales, waited for the digital display to go back to zero, then as gently as she could, stepped back on.

She bit her lip and peered down at the flickering digital numbers. When the numbers stopped moving, her heart sank.

Crap. She gained a whole two pounds since last week. How was that even possible?

She kicked the scales with her foot, and they skidded across the bathroom floor, hitting the wall with a crash. It was that bloody triple-chocolate brownie she'd eaten last night. What on earth possessed her?

Oh, but it tasted so good.

All the dieting articles in magazines she read lately said you should only weigh yourself once a week. They mentioned water fluctuations or something like that. Maybe that was it?

No, she was kidding herself. It had to be the brownie. Now, she would be in a bad mood all day.

She reached for her toothbrush and began performing side leg lifts as she squeezed out some whitening toothpaste. The exercises had been part of her morning ritual for as long as she could remember.

She began to scrub her teeth and wobbled a little as she tried to balance on one foot. She would give anything not to worry about her weight. Why couldn't she be one of those naturally slim dancers like Anya?

At the thought of her friend, Victoria smiled. Lucky cow. Bet she was having a fab time of it, hobnobbing with the rich guests on the cruise liner. Victoria sighed. What a brilliant way to see the world.

She was surprised Anya hadn't told her brother about her new job. He seemed genuinely worried about her, and Victoria couldn't help feeling sorry for him. Okay, he was overprotective, but he cared about Anya, at least.

Victoria couldn't say the same for her family. She doubted they would notice.

Victoria spat the toothpaste out and rinsed her mouth. She felt guilty not telling Henryk where Anya had gone, especially when he looked at her with those sad, grey eyes, but she promised Anya she wouldn't tell a soul, and a promise was a promise. And now her loyalty had paid off big time.

Victoria smiled. Just this morning she'd had an exciting

phone call about an audition for a cruise ship. The American man on the phone said Anya recommended her personally. Good old Anya. It might not be the West End, but it was a step in the right direction.

After she finished brushing her teeth, Victoria reached for her pot of Johnson's twenty-four hour, sweat-resistant body makeup. She started to dab it over the scars on her arms. It didn't cover the marks completely, so she always wore long sleeves, but the makeup gave her that extra little bit of confidence. And confidence was definitely necessary in her chosen profession. Around every corner, there were people ready and waiting to knock you down.

Victoria always got up, dusted herself off and carried on. She had already gone through too much to give up on her dreams.

Those daydreams helped her through some very difficult times in her childhood. When things got really bad, she would close her eyes and picture her name in lights, which always helped. Having something to focus on, to look forward to, really made a difference.

Victoria rifled though her makeup bag and pulled out her eyeliner. She stuck her tongue out as she drew a line across her top lashes, concentrating on getting it straight. She had to look perfect today. She glanced down at her stomach. Shame about those extra two pounds.

An hour later, Victoria wrapped her long-sleeved cardigan tightly around her waist and walked into the wind. It was a warm morning, but this alleyway was a wind trap. Hell, it was making her eyes water. She was going to turn up at the audition looking a right state.

She felt a flutter of panic building in her stomach. She didn't even know what she would have to do for this audition. The man on the phone didn't tell her whether they wanted a singer or a dancer, and she'd been too overwhelmed by the phone call to ask sensible questions. She hoped it was a dancer they needed. Singing wasn't her strongest point, but she was taking lessons, trying to improve.

Victoria tugged at her sleeves, making sure they came right down to her wrists. Think positive, she ordered herself. She'd be all right. Of course, they would want her. They might even offer her the job on the spot. She smiled and drifted off to a daydream where she was the most famous dancer in the world, where she would be in such high demand that…

Damn. Victoria caught sight of her reflection in a shop window. She sucked her stomach in. That bloody brownie had added at least an inch to her waist. No dinner tonight, that was for sure.

When Victoria left the alleyway, she looked around in surprise. She didn't know this area. It didn't look like the sort of place to have a theatre or a studio. In fact, the buildings around here looked abandoned.

She looked down at the piece of paper in her hand where she had quickly jotted down the man's instructions. She must have made a wrong turn. This couldn't be it, surely. She read through the directions again, then she shrugged. She hadn't made a mistake. She'd followed his directions perfectly.

She walked on, passing an old, red brick wall that was crumbling with age. The noise from the traffic, now several streets away, was a muffled hum. Victoria's confident smile faded. The moaning wind blew a few yellow leaves past her feet, and Victoria shivered as the sun slipped behind a cloud.

She continued up to the old, grey stone building, which according to her hastily scrawled notes, was her destination. The building was surrounded by a mesh fence. Victoria blinked up at the dark windows. This couldn't be where they were holding the auditions. It didn't feel right. The building looked as if it had been marked for demolition.

A fluttering movement caught the corner of Victoria's eye. A white sign, attached to the fence with a plastic cable tie, moved in the breeze. Victoria walked forward and grabbed it to stop the sign blowing upside down.

The word "Auditions" was printed in black capital letters next to an arrow, which pointed to a pathway along the side of the building.

There was a small gap in the fence. Victoria squeezed her way through, hitched her bag up onto her shoulder and set off down the path, which was scattered with dead leaves and straggly weeds. Victoria quickened her pace.

At the end of the trail, she stopped and looked up at the back of the huge building. Then a movement and a slapping noise sent Victoria's heart pounding.

She was ready to run when she saw it was only a startled pigeon. She shook her head, and tried to laugh it off. Why was she so jittery? It was only an old building. She looked at it again. See, she told herself, it's just a pile of old bricks, nothing to be scared of.

She walked closer, moving towards the cracked, stone steps that led up to what must once have been a grand entrance. She shrugged. What did it matter what the building looked like? It wouldn't make any difference to her audition.

Victoria plastered on her performance smile, opened the door and walked through the arched doorway.

CHAPTER TWELVE

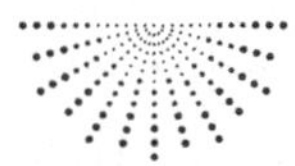

ON THE POSITIVE SIDE, Mackinnon's nose didn't hurt that much, but unfortunately, he looked as if he'd gone ten rounds with Mike Tyson.

"What the hell happened to you?" Collins asked when Mackinnon walked into the open plan office at Wood Street Police Station.

Mackinnon's hand automatically went to touch his nose, and he winced.

"Christ, did Chloe do that?"

"No, of course she didn't," Mackinnon said. "Don't be ridiculous."

"Oh." Collins raised an eyebrow. "Walked into a door, did you?"

"As a matter of fact… Oh, forget it. Is DI Green in yet?"

"Yes, but he's in a meeting with the superintendent."

Mackinnon frowned. That didn't sound good. In fact,

Mackinnon was pretty sure it meant this case was going to be taken off their hands sooner, rather than later. Mackinnon picked up his coat again.

"Are you not staying?" Collins asked.

"I'm going to check out the coffee shop where Anya worked."

"Now? But I thought we were going to do that..."

"Better to do it now," Mackinnon said. "Rather than wait to hear the superintendent has reassigned the case to MIT officers only."

"He wouldn't," Collins said with feeling.

"Of course, he will, Nick. It's not just a missing persons case anymore. Henryk Blonski has been murdered."

Mackinnon left before Collins could argue. It was ridiculous to think the super would be happy for them to plod on with the case. It would be assigned to the Major Investigation Team as soon as officers were available.

Anya Blonski worked at a branch of Starbucks on Cheapside. Cheapside used to be the main market in the City of London. Streets nearby had names like Poultry Street. Bread Street and Milk Street. They were all named after the goods that used to be sold there. In the last few years, the whole area had been completely redeveloped, with a fancy shopping mall and restaurants owned by celebrity chefs taking up the old market space. But the old street names remained, including Wood Street, where the headquarters of the City of London Police was located.

Mackinnon often walked past the coffee shop where Anya worked, but he had never been inside.

The coffee shop was set out in a standard way. Wooden

tables and chairs took up the middle area of the shop floor, and grey velvet-covered sofas and armchairs were set back against the walls. It was quiet when he entered. There were only two tables occupied and no one waiting to be served.

The guy behind the counter wore a black polo shirt under a green apron. He was almost bald, save a few stray, fair strands. Despite that, Mackinnon guessed the man was only mid-twenties. He looked up as Mackinnon approached.

"Hey, what can I get you?"

Mackinnon showed his warrant card and the employee's smile slipped off his face.

He swallowed. "Is this something to do with Anya?"

Mackinnon waited for a moment, to see what else he might say. Sometimes, if you let them, people would volunteer more information on their own. Questions often made people clam up, even if they had nothing to hide.

But the man behind the counter didn't say anything else. He picked up a marker pen and fiddled with it.

If something *had* happened to Anya, nine times out of ten, the person responsible would be someone she knew.

"Yes, it's about Anya Blonski," Mackinnon said. "I'll need to talk to you and the rest of the staff."

He nodded. "Of course." He left the counter and poked his head around the door behind him.

Another customer entered the shop, a woman in a sharp business suit.

"Mind if we do this one at a time?" the man said, nodding at the customer.

"Sure."

A heavy-set girl came out of the door behind the counter, carrying two large cartons of milk. She had thick, dark eyebrows, which almost met in the middle when she looked at Mackinnon and frowned.

The man asked, "Can you cover?"

She nodded.

They headed over to a table while the girl served the customer.

"What's your name?" Mackinnon asked.

"Jim... Jim Meadows. Has something happened to Anya?"

Mackinnon waited.

"I only ask because she hasn't shown up for her shifts, and her brother was in here on Wednesday asking after her. He seemed really worried."

"Wednesday? What time was that?"

"In the morning. Around eleven. Anya didn't show up for her shift. She was supposed to start at eight thirty."

"How long have you known Anya?" Mackinnon asked.

Jim Meadows shrugged. "Around ten months. Since she started working here."

"Did you get on well?"

"Sure. I mean we don't socialise out of work, but she's a nice girl."

"Did she confide in you? Tell you anything about her personal life?"

"How do you mean?"

"She's a pretty girl. Did any of the customers go a little too far with their flirting? Or did she have problems with a boyfriend?" Mackinnon kept his expression friendly.

Jim shook his head. "She never mentioned a boyfriend. I think she was too caught up in all that performing arts stuff."

"Performing arts? You mean her dancing?"

"Yes. She takes classes." Jim Meadows smiled with a dreamy expression on his face. "I reckon she'd make a good dancer. She'll probably be on TV one day. Or in a show in the West End. You know, then I can say I knew her before she was famous…"

Mackinnon nodded and waited for him to continue.

"She has this kind of grace about her. She's beautiful."

"That must attract a bit of attention around here."

Jim shrugged. "Well, sure. But she's oblivious to it. Never seems to notice."

"So there were no regular customers who flirted with her?"

Jim Meadows thought for a moment. "A couple maybe, but I don't think there's anything in it." He rested his elbows on the table and leaned forward. "The worst flirts are the married ones."

"Really?"

Jim nodded. "They come in with their rings clearly visible on their fingers and flirt like crazy. But they do that with Milly as well." Jim turned behind him to face Milly at the counter. Her bushy eyebrows lowered as she scowled at them. "Like I said, there's nothing in it."

"When was the last time you saw Anya?"

"Tuesday, when she worked her normal morning shift. She likes to keep her afternoons free for her dance classes."

"Did you ever meet any of her friends from those dance classes?"

"No, she doesn't really talk about them either. I mean, she talks about the classes, but not about any of her friends there. I get the impression she doesn't make friends all that easily."

"But you like her?"

"Yes. She is a sweet girl."

Mackinnon took a few more details from Jim Meadows. He wrote down the name of the performing arts school Anya attended, which matched the information Collins had already unearthed yesterday.

Jim Meadows watched Mackinnon note down the address.

"I think we're done for now," Mackinnon said. "Could you ask Milly to come over next?"

Jim Meadows pushed back his chair, licked his lips, then said, "Do you think something has happened to Anya? Her brother seemed really worried."

"I'm sorry to have to tell you this, but Anya's brother, Henryk Blonski, was killed."

Jim Meadows clapped a hand over his mouth.

"We are still trying to locate Anya."

Jim Meadows blinked rapidly. "Oh, God. Poor Anya." He stood up and walked back to the counter.

Mackinnon watched his reaction carefully. The shock, the emotion, could it all be an act? One thing was for sure, Jim Meadows liked Anya. Did he like her too much?

Milly bustled over, wiping her hands on her green apron. She sat down and didn't wait for Mackinnon to speak first.

"I'm sure I can't tell you anything that will help," she said, crossing her arms. "I wasn't exactly close to Anya."

"I'd like you to tell me what you can about Anya."

"What do you want to know?"

Mackinnon leaned forward. "Tell me everything. I want to know everything."

CHAPTER THIRTEEN

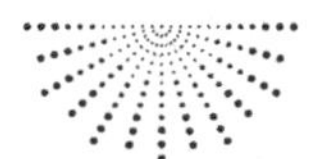

WHEN MACKINNON GOT BACK to the station, he headed straight over to Collins' desk. Collins had been working with a Polish translator to break the news to the Blonski family back in Poland. Collins' face showed the strain.

"You managed to get in touch with the parents?" Mackinnon asked.

Collins nodded. "Yes, through the Polish *Policja*."

Collins nodded in the direction of the door. "DI Green wanted you to update him as soon as you got back."

Mackinnon nodded and shrugged off his jacket. "I'll go and see him now. You coming?"

Collins shook his head. "I've already seen him."

The heating was on in DI Green's office, despite the fact it was July and London was in the middle of a heat wave, with temperatures hovering around the ninety-degree mark during the day.

DI Green appeared immune to the heat. He invited Mackinnon to take a seat and listened as Mackinnon filled him in as quickly as he could.

When Mackinnon finished, DI Green nodded slowly and pulled the red plant pot, containing a squat cactus, on his desk towards him, peering down at it.

"I had a spider plant before this one," DI Green said. "I thought a cactus might be easier to look after, but it's not looking good."

Mackinnon looked at the spiky plant. He didn't know much about cacti, but it looked all right to him.

"The thing is, Jack," DI Green said, leaning back in his chair and linking his hands together behind his head, "I've got some bad news."

Mackinnon waited for him to continue.

"I suppose you've heard about the incident at the Towers Estate?" Without waiting for an answer, DI Green continued. "There's a hostage situation, and MIT are snowed under at the moment, which means it's still me heading up the Blonski case for now."

Mackinnon nodded.

"It won't be for too much longer, just until MIT get the situation under control. So that means you and Collins are going to be doing a lot of the leg work today."

Mackinnon didn't mind that at all. He wanted to move to MIT, and he knew Collins had similar ambitions. "Just tell me what you need us to do, sir."

DI Green smiled, opened his desk drawer and pulled out a list.

After he'd finished with DI Green, Mackinnon found Collins grabbing a coffee from the vending machine.

"So what did DI Green say?" Collins asked. "Did you have a nice chat about how I royally messed up?"

"What? No, of course not," Mackinnon said. "He gave me a list of things we need to do."

"Well, when I went to see him, he was definitely hinting I screwed up. And he wasn't very subtle about it."

"You're being paranoid, Nick."

"Really? Well, it sounded like that to me. He went on for ages. 'Why on earth haven't you done this yet? Do I have to think of everything myself?'" Collins said, mimicking the detective inspector and putting on a voice uncannily like DI Green's.

Mackinnon had to smile.

"He thinks it's my fault, Jack."

Mackinnon shook his head.

"He does," Collins insisted. "He's been looking at me like I screwed up, like I missed it."

"Nick, you haven't missed anything, but if you don't get a grip, we might do."

Collins took at deep breath, then nodded. "Yeah, right. Sorry. So what did you find out at the coffee shop?"

"Jim Meadows. He works with Anya at Starbucks, and I think he had a thing for her."

"Yeah?" Collins brightened. "Fancy him for it?"

"Too early to say, but he's one to watch."

Collins took a couple of gulps of coffee, then sighed. "She'd only been missing a day, Jack. How was I supposed to know? I'm not bloody psychic."

Mackinnon could keep telling Collins it wasn't his fault until he was blue in the face. It wouldn't make any difference. Collins had to work it through for himself.

"Jim also mentioned the dance classes Anya attended. We need to check out this dance academy place as a priority."

Collins nodded. "All right. What about Henryk's place of work?"

Mackinnon nodded. "We can split up, cover more ground. Which would you prefer? Academy or Henryk's work place?"

"I think it might be better if we check out this dance place together. Then we can check out the bar where Henryk Blonski worked."

"All right." Mackinnon picked up his coat. He wouldn't say anything yet. Collins didn't want to go alone because he'd lost his confidence. It wasn't DI Green who was blaming Collins for missing something. Collins was doing an excellent job of that all by himself.

CHAPTER FOURTEEN

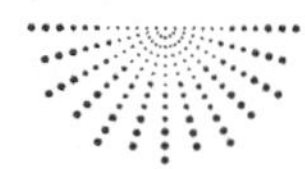

VICTORIA HEARD THE HINGES on the door squeal, then the heavy wooden door slammed shut behind her.

This was a creepy place. She couldn't wait to finish the audition so she could get the hell out of here. She waited in what looked like a reception hall for a few moments, as her eyes adjusted to the dim light. She glanced upwards at the vaulted ceiling. There were no lights on.

There was a desk near the door, but no phone, or computer. She moved over to the desk and touched it with her index finger, leaving a trail in the dust.

She had to be in the wrong place. This was seriously freaking her out. Why didn't she ask for the man's number when he called? She realised her mistake and dialled 1471, but that hadn't helped as the telephone number had been withheld.

She walked a little further into the large hall, her footsteps echoing against the chipped, dirty tiles. She spotted another door at the other end of the hall. She decided to have a quick look inside. If no one were there, she'd go home, run a hot bath and write off the audition. There would be other chances.

She strode across the hall to the mystery door, twisted the handle and pushed. It didn't budge. Victoria exhaled the breath she'd been holding and let her hand slip from the handle. That was it then, time to admit defeat and go home.

"Victoria?"

Victoria whirled around, her heart hammering, but she couldn't see anyone. God, calm down. It was okay, she reassured herself. It was the man she'd spoken to on the phone. She recognised his American accent.

"I'm in the entrance hall," Victoria called out and turned in a slow circle, looking for the source of the voice. "I thought I'd gotten the wrong place."

"Yes, I suppose it must seem an odd place to meet." The voice came from directly behind her.

Startled, Victoria turned. She struggled to keep her lips curved in a polite smile.

The man stepped out of the shadows, and she saw him properly for the first time.

"Oh, it's you… What are you doing here?" Confusion played over Victoria's face.

The man put on his phoney American accent and drawled, "Well, aren't you pleased to see me?"

Victoria's eyes widened. "It was you on the phone. Why? What are you playing at?"

She spun around, looking for TV cameras. She half expected people to jump out at her, laughing. Maybe this was a new show like "You've been framed."

But there was no one else here.

She began to nod slowly, the pieces falling into place. She got it now. This was the famous casting couch. He expected to have his way with her, then…

Well, he could think again. She didn't need to do things like that to be a success. She'd make it without going through any of that crap.

He grinned at her, showing his pointed teeth. He tapped something in his hand. What was that? What was he hiding? Victoria's heart started to pound. Her eyes shot to the exit.

"I'm leaving," she said, turning on her heel.

"Not so soon. You'll hurt my feelings."

He moved so fast, she didn't have time to react. She felt a sharp scratch on her neck.

"Ow! What the hell?" She looked up at his face. A face so familiar, but today, it seemed different. It seemed menacing, evil.

She blinked. His face melted away in front of her eyes.

He caught her just as her knees buckled.

"Just relax," he whispered. "I've got you."

CHAPTER FIFTEEN

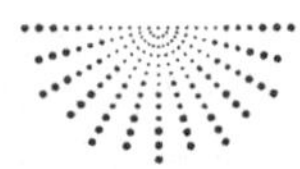

THE STAR ACADEMY TOOK up the top three floors of an old, red-brick, Georgian building on Western Lane. In the weak sunlight, the building looked every bit its age. The decorative stonework had crumbled and hadn't been repaired. Maybe it had been an impressive building once, but its glory days were now long gone.

The ground floor of the building was taken up by a glass-fronted furniture store called Oakland's. An oak table and chairs took up pride of place in the display window.

Collins rang the bell set next to a small sign with Star Academy embossed in gold letters. No one answered. After waiting for a few moments, Collins jabbed at the bell again.

Mackinnon and Collins stood back as two young girls barrelled out of the door, laughing. Mackinnon caught the door before it swung shut behind them. Mackinnon and Collins entered the tired-looking lobby. A receptionist sat behind a small desk.

They caught the receptionist mid-yawn. She smothered it with one hand and anxiously pushed her nail file out of sight with the other hand.

"How can I help?" She smiled up at them.

"We'd like to speak to the owner of the academy." Collins held up his ID. "Police."

The receptionist's eyes widened.

"Oh, right," she said and reached for the phone. "Just a moment."

Mackinnon picked up a glossy brochure from the reception desk. The front cover claimed Star Academy could help you reach for the stars. Mackinnon flicked through pages describing the different dancing, singing and acting classes the academy had to offer, and then read the "about us" page at the back of the brochure. Apparently, the academy was formed by members of the multi-award winning Cleeves family three years ago. A list of testimonials, declaring Madame Cleeves to be a genius, appeared beneath the main body of the text.

The snazzy sales description in bright pink letters told him the Star Academy was open only to females, and classes held a maximum of ten students.

The receptionist pushed back on her black, wheeled, office chair, then walked around the desk. "If you would like to follow me, please, gentlemen, I will take you to Mr. And Mrs. Cleeves. Sorry, I mean Madame Cleeves. She doesn't like to be called Mrs."

Mackinnon exchanged a look with Collins.

"I'm babbling, aren't I? Sorry."

"Not at all," Mackinnon said. "What's your name?"

"Pippa Adams." The receptionist ducked her head shyly.

"How long have you worked here, Pippa?" Mackinnon asked as the receptionist led them upstairs and along a narrow corridor.

"Two years," Pippa said and gave them a nervous smile.

They walked on past classes that were underway. All the doors were shut, but Mackinnon could hear one that definitely sounded like a tap class. Another had flashing, coloured lights shining through the gap underneath the door. He didn't have a clue what that class might be for.

As they neared the end of the corridor, the sound of piano music drifted towards them, a simple, repetitive tune. The receptionist stopped in front of a green-panelled door, rapped against the wood, then opened it and stuck her head in the room.

"I'm very sorry, Madame–" the receptionist said.

Mackinnon couldn't see inside, but heard the high, thin voice of a woman reply, "For goodness sake! How many times do I have to tell you? Never interrupt a class in progress."

The tentative smile slipped from the receptionist's face. "I am sorry, Madame, but–"

"Go away!"

Mackinnon pushed the door open fully and stepped past the receptionist.

"Mrs. Cleeves?"

A tiny woman stood in the middle of the room. Her dark brown hair was scraped back in a bun, and she stood, hands on her hips, glaring at Mackinnon.

She stepped forward. "And who are you?"

"Detective Sergeant Mackinnon." Mackinnon gestured to Collins. "And Detective Constable Collins of the City of London Police. "We would like a word with you and your husband, please."

The woman scowled, wrinkles trailing out from her screwed up mouth. Mackinnon guessed she was a long-term smoker.

She wore ballet tights and a leotard and was very slim, not an ounce of body fat to be seen anywhere.

From her face, Mackinnon would have put her age at around sixty, but her body was almost childlike. She reminded him of a sparrow. A really angry sparrow.

Mackinnon towered over her. She couldn't have been more than five feet, but she held herself with a regal stance. Her perfume was oriental, spicy and too strong. Mackinnon resisted the urge to take a step back.

A man sitting at the piano stood up with a wince. "I'm Roger. Roger Cleeves. This is my wife, Belinda. How can we help?"

"We'd like to ask you a few questions about Anya Blonski," Mackinnon said. "I understand she is a student here."

Belinda crossed her arms and tutted. "She *was* a student here."

"Not anymore?"

Belinda tapped her foot in irritation and scowled. "No, not anymore. She left."

"Why did she leave?" Collins asked. "Do you know where she went?"

"Of course, I know where she went. The selfish little opportunist. She had a better offer, didn't she? Got a job as an entertainer on one of these cruise liners." She shook her head. "Such a waste. She did have talent, you know. She just needed to work on her classical technique. But she wasn't interested in work. Like the rest of them, she wanted it handed to her on a plate. They run off to these cruise ships, expecting to become stars overnight."

"I'm sorry," Roger Cleeves said. "My wife is a little upset. Anya left, and I think she may have owed us money for tuition."

"No," Belinda said. "That's the ridiculous thing. She had paid up for another term only two days before she left."

Roger turned to his wife. "I didn't realise."

"Doesn't that strike you as odd?" Mackinnon asked.

"Well, yes," Roger Cleeves said. "It does seem rather unusual."

Belinda Cleeves frowned. "I suppose she just changed her mind. These girls can be very flighty." She tapped a skinny finger against her temple. "Who knows what goes on in their heads?"

"Did you know Anya's brother?"

"No. Not really." Belinda shook her head. "He met Anya after she finished class a couple of times, but I never actually spoke to him until after Anya left us. He came to see us on Wednesday. It seems she ran off without even telling her poor brother where she was going."

"You saw Henryk Blonski on Wednesday?" Mackinnon said, anticipation rising. "What time was this?"

"Oh, now let me see," Roger Cleeves said. "It would have been mid-morning. Perhaps ten thirty. He wanted to ask us all if we knew which cruise company Anya was working for."

Collins dropped his pencil on the floor. He was on edge.

"And which company is she working for?" he asked, barely hiding the frustration in his voice.

"That's just it," Roger Cleeves said. "None of us knew."

Mackinnon paused for a moment, then said. "Did Anya tell you she was leaving?"

"No, she didn't," Belinda said. "Ungrateful wretch. I heard it from one of the other students. Everyone was talking about it on Wednesday."

"And do you remember which student told you?"

Belinda paused. "No, I don't." She turned to her husband. "Do you remember, Roger?"

Roger Cleeves shook his head slowly. "You told me she left, but I can't recall who mentioned it to you first."

There was a small crack as the tip of Collins' pencil broke against his notebook. "Where were you both on Wednesday night?"

"Wednesday night?" Belinda repeated. "I don't see it's any business of yours."

"We are working on a murder inquiry here. I don't have time to play games," Collins snapped. "Just answer the question."

Mackinnon shot him a warning look, which Collins ignored.

"Well?" Collins asked. "What were you doing on Wednesday night?"

"Murder inquiry?" Belinda pressed a hand to her chest. "Oh God. You mean Anya…?"

Roger put an arm around his wife.

"Not Anya," Collins said. "Henryk."

Belinda and Roger Cleeves both looked confused.

"Let me see," Roger Cleeves said. "After our classes, we

shut up the academy at eight, and we stayed in all night, apart from my nightly constitutional. We ate dinner with our children at eight thirty. Then I went out for my walk about nine thirty, and I was back within forty-five minutes."

Collins nodded, then looked around the dance studio. "Quite a big place you have here. How many students?"

"Now, let me see," Roger Cleeves said. "I've forgotten the exact number, but it's around eighty."

"And they all attend part time?"

"Mostly, yes."

"And if you don't mind me asking, what sort of qualifications do you need to set up a place like this? Or don't you need any?"

Belinda Cleeves' face twitched in irritation. "I happen to be a former ballerina, Detective. I toured all over the world. Our son, Nathan, used to be part of a boy band called Vivid." She paused. "You must have heard of them. They were hugely influential."

Mackinnon was about to say he hadn't when Collins nodded. "Yeah. Boy band. Early nineties."

"Not just a boy band, Detective. They made history with their beautiful songs." Belinda Cleeves said. "They won six Brit awards, you know?"

"Really?" Collins said, sounding bored.

"Yes, and they were almost signed by Simon Cowell. My husband used to work with Simon, you know. He worked in the industry for years. I assure you, our qualifications are more than adequate."

Roger Cleeves patted his wife's hand. "Come now, darling, I'm sure the detectives didn't come here to discuss Nathan's career."

Mackinnon took the lead on the rest of the questions. He could see Collins was close to losing his temper with Mr. and Mrs. Cleeves.

Over the next few minutes, Belinda Cleeves became increasingly distracted and started shouting out remarks to her dancers. Mackinnon decided they had gotten as much help as they were going to get from this pair and asked if they could speak to any other teachers who worked with Anya.

"There are only two other teachers. "My son, Nathan, and my daughter, Rachel."

"So it's a family business?" Collins asked.

"It is. I wouldn't trust anyone else to share my vision," she said in a cold voice.

CHAPTER SIXTEEN

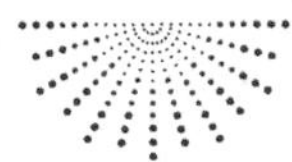

NATHAN CLEEVES PUFFED OUT his chest and strode towards Mackinnon and Collins. He was attempting to look intimidating, but Mackinnon found it hard to be intimidated by a man wearing skin-coloured tights.

Collins shot Mackinnon a startled glance. "Christ. He's not shy, is he?"

Mackinnon kept his eyes above Nathan's chest.

"You've interrupted the class," Nathan Cleeves said, his nostrils flaring. "I hope this is important."

"I consider murder important, Mr. Cleeves," Mackinnon said. "Don't you?"

Nathan Cleeves' dark eyes darted between Mackinnon and Collins. "Murder? What murder?" His voice was less confrontational, but he kept the sneer.

"A young man, name of Henryk Blonski," Collins said. "Do you know him?"

"Henryk Blonski." Nathan Cleeves blinked rapidly. "Anya's brother?"

Mackinnon nodded.

Nathan looked down at the floor. His shock seemed genuine. "Why would anyone want to kill him?"

"That's what we want to find out," Collins said. "Did you know he was looking into Anya's disappearance?"

"Anya left." Nathan Cleeves glared at Mackinnon, daring him to contradict. He jutted out his chin. "She's gone off to work on a cruise ship. Stupid girl. Now, she'll never amount to anything."

"Why do you say that?" Collins asked.

"She couldn't take the pace." Nathan shrugged. "She wasn't prepared to put in the work. She's a quitter. The type of person who is always looking for the easy way out. I mean, a cruise ship, for God's sake."

Nathan snorted and shook his head. "Pathetic."

"Did you have a relationship with Anya Blonski?" Collins asked. "She was a pretty girl. You must have noticed."

"What?" Nathan jerked his head around to face Collins. "As if."

"You sound bitter." Collins said. "Did she turn you down?"

A cold smile stretched across Nathan Cleeves' face. "I can assure you, Detective, I have no trouble getting attention from women. No trouble, at all."

Mackinnon was getting tired of this. "Did you have a relationship with Anya Blonski, yes or no?"

"No," Nathan scowled. "She took a ballet class with me

twice a week. I didn't socialise with her outside the academy."

"And Henryk Blonski," Mackinnon said. "How well did you know him?"

Nathan ran a hand through his floppy, black hair. "I'd seen him around, waiting for Anya after class a couple of times. But I'd never spoken to him until after Anya left. He came here asking questions about her. I guess Anya didn't tell him her plans."

"Where were you on Wednesday night, Mr. Cleeves?" Collins asked.

Nathan shook his head. "Unbelievable. You're all the bloody same. If you must know, I was here until about nine pm. I had dinner here, then I went out."

"And who did you go out with?"

"A woman." Nathan Cleeves leered at Collins. "From the look of you, I don't suppose you get a lot of female company, do you?"

Collins took out his notepad. "Is this woman your girlfriend?"

Nathan shrugged. "For now."

Mackinnon imagined the satisfaction he'd get from slapping the smirk off Nathan Cleeves' face. He was impressed that Collins managed to keep his cool.

"Name and address of your girlfriend, please, Mr. Cleeves," Mackinnon said. "We'd like to speak to her."

Nathan recited the name and address with the smile of a man who knew he had a perfect alibi.

"Are we done here? I do have a class to teach." Nathan Cleeves gestured to the collection of dancers limbering up at the far end of the studio.

Mackinnon watched them for a moment. How was it possible for the human body to be so flexible?

"Go ahead," Mackinnon said. "We'll need to speak to your sister, though; Rachel, isn't it?"

Nathan gave a disinterested shrug. "All right."

He waved at his father, who was sitting by the piano. The old man eased himself off the stool with a wince, then hobbled towards them.

"They want to talk to Rachel," Nathan said to his father. Then he turned to walk away, muttering, "God knows why."

"Ah, of course," Roger Cleeves said. "Rachel's taking a singing class at the moment." He glanced at his watch. "But I think she may have just finished. If you'd like to follow me, I'll take you to her classroom."

CHAPTER SEVENTEEN

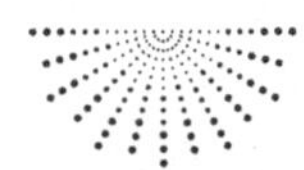

ROGER CLEEVES LED MACKINNON and Collins out of the dance studio and down a long, narrow corridor.

"Are you okay, sir?" Collins asked, looking down at Roger Cleeves' legs as the man limped along in front of them.

"Fine," Roger Cleeves said. "I'm used to it. Just a touch of arthritis. My knee gets a bit stiff after I've been sitting down for a while."

He pushed open a white door leading to the stairwell and gestured for Mackinnon and Collins to go ahead of him. "Rachel's classroom is on the second floor. I'll let you go in front. It takes me a while." He grinned ruefully and began to climb the steps, following Mackinnon and Collins.

They took the stairs slowly, but still had to wait for Roger Cleeves when they reached the landing. He kept his left leg outstretched, which gave him a strange gait as he climbed the stairs.

"Sorry to keep you," he muttered, grasping the banister.

Mackinnon frowned. "Not a problem, sir. I appreciate you showing us the way."

Mackinnon couldn't help thinking what a selfish bastard the man's son was. Surely, Nathan could have shown them the way instead and saved his father the painful walk.

"I'm sorry my wife was a little abrupt before," Roger Cleeves said as he reached the top of the stairs and sighed with relief. "She's more upset than she lets on. She really did see star quality in Anya, and she was very disappointed when Anya left."

They exited the stairwell and walked along another corridor almost identical to the one downstairs. The sound of someone singing scales drifted toward them.

Roger Cleeves stopped at the first door they came to and rapped on the frosted glass panel. He opened the door a crack and poked his head inside.

The singing stopped.

"Can we have a word, sweetheart?"

Mackinnon didn't hear a response, but it was obvious Roger Cleeves did. He pushed the door wide open and waved Mackinnon and Collins into the room.

The two women in the room turned, wide-eyed with curiosity.

"Rachel, darling," Roger Cleeves said and beckoned her over. "This is DS Mackinnon and DC Collins. They want to ask you a few questions about Anya."

The shorter of the two women tucked her light brown hair behind her ears and ran a hand along the buttons of her cardigan.

"That will be all for today, Roxie," she said in a reedy, tremulous voice.

Mackinnon turned his attention to Roxie. Her bottle-blonde hair was scraped back in a high ponytail. She pouted her bubblegum-pink lips and sashayed towards the door, staring at Mackinnon and Collins with blatant interest.

It was hard to see how the contrast between the two women could have been greater. Compared to the highly-coloured, flamboyant Roxie, Rachel looked pale and drab.

Rachel's eyes flickered up to meet Mackinnon's gaze. She blinked rapidly then looked back down at the floor.

"Oh, all right." Rachel Cleeves played with the cuff of her cardigan, which was several sizes too big for her. "Although, I'm sure I can't tell you anything useful," she said with a slight lisp.

Her beige, baggy cardigan was worn over a faded, old-fashioned tea dress. Brown, clumpy shoes finished off her outfit.

"I'll leave you to it then," Roger Cleeves said, cheerfully. "Take them back downstairs to reception when you're finished, Rachel."

Rachel nodded.

As Roger Cleeves closed the door behind him, Rachel turned to look at Mackinnon and Collins in turn before looking down at the desk in front of her.

"Please, have a seat," she said and gestured to the wooden desks, which were set out in a classroom fashion.

Mackinnon and Collins sat down at desks in the front row.

They must have been designed for primary-school children, Mackinnon thought as he tried to fit his long legs under the desk. He couldn't quite manage it and had to leave one leg in the aisle.

That seemed to amuse Rachel Cleeves. "Sorry, they are a little on the small side." A ghost of a smile played on her lips for a few moments before it disappeared.

"I understand you taught Anya," Collins said.

"That's right. She had singing lessons twice a week."

"Was she any good?"

Rachel paused, frowned, then said, "She was okay, but I think dancing was her real talent."

Mackinnon leaned forward, trying to get comfortable behind the tiny desk. "Were you close? Did she confide in you?"

Rachel and Anya were similar in age. On the surface, it seemed like they had little in common, but you never knew…

"Close?" Rachel said the word as if it puzzled her. "No, we weren't close."

Rachel kept her eyes fixed on her hands in her lap. Mackinnon was starting to find her inability to maintain eye contact maddening.

"She didn't tell you she was leaving?" Collins asked.

Rachel licked her lips and shook her head. "She didn't tell me herself, no. But I heard a rumour she accepted a job on a cruise ship." She said the final words in a disdainful tone.

"You don't approve of cruise ships?" Mackinnon asked with a smile.

"It's not the cruise ships I don't approve of," she said as she tucked her mousy hair behind her ears again. "These days, everyone wants to be famous for being famous. Most of our students don't come to the academy because they love music or want to be on the stage. They just want to be in the gossip mags." She rolled her eyes. "Two of our ex-students have been on Big Brother, you know?" She shook her head as if that said it all.

"Is that what Anya wanted?" Mackinnon asked. "To be famous?"

Rachel bit her thumbnail. "It's funny because Anya… Well, Anya didn't seem that way to me. I thought she was different, but I guess, you never can tell."

Rachel stared down at the floor.

"Who told you about Anya's job on the cruise ship?" Mackinnon asked.

"Oh." Rachel bit her lower lip. "I can't remember. There were a few people chatting about it in my class yesterday. I'm not sure who mentioned it first." She shrugged. "I just remember thinking my mother would be furious."

"Did anyone mention the name of the cruise ship? The operators?"

Rachel shook her head. "Not that I remember."

"Rachel," Mackinnon said, "how well do you know Henryk Blonski?"

"I don't know him at all. I only met him once. He came here on Wednesday to ask if I could tell him which cruise ship Anya signed up with. Why?"

"Henryk Blonski was found dead this morning."

Rachel paled.

"Can you describe your movements on Wednesday night?" Collins said.

"My movements?" Rachel Cleeves ran a hand across her

skirt, smoothing it over her thighs. "I was at home." She pointed upstairs. "We live in a flat on the third floor."

"With your parents?" Collins asked.

A flicker of irritation passed over Rachel's face. "Yes. Nathan and I live with our parents. It's a large flat and accommodation is extremely expensive in London."

"So you didn't go out at all on Wednesday night?" Collins asked.

"No, Detective. I was here all night."

Rachel escorted them back to reception in silence. She was pissed off with them, but Mackinnon didn't care. It wasn't his job to be likeable, and there was something strange about the Cleeves family.

After Rachel Cleeves had shown Mackinnon and Collins the door, Mackinnon stepped out onto the street, turned to Collins and said, "What did you make of them?"

Collins screwed up his face and looked up at the exterior of the Star Academy. "Bunch of weirdos."

"That's your professional opinion, is it?" Mackinnon asked, moving out of the way as a woman, weighed down by shopping bags, pushed past them.

"Nathan Cleeves," Collins said, screwing up his face as though he'd bitten into a lemon. "I'm going to check up on him."

"We'll need to run a check on all of them. Shall we pop in while we're here?" Mackinnon nodded at the furniture store next to the academy.

"Shopping?" Collins asked.

Mackinnon pointed at the huge glass windows. "Good view of the street. Staff working in here may have seen

Anya now and then. They may have seen something important."

Mackinnon pushed open the shop door, and a bell tinkled as they entered the store.

There were no customers or staff. Mackinnon glanced around the surprisingly large shop.

It was one of those places with beautiful, polished wood floors, and smooth, handmade furniture that reminded Mackinnon of his grandparents' house. The smell of freshly cut wood took him back in time to his grandfather's workshop with its rows of tools, planes and files, and curly wood shavings.

Oak bed frames, wardrobes, chairs and tables were scattered around the shop floor in no discernible order. Mackinnon picked up a red cardboard "for sale" sign from a rocking chair. Everything had little red stickers, advertising final reductions.

"Good choice, sir. That's a fine, handmade rocker. Top quality," a voice behind them said. Mackinnon turned to see a plump, middle-aged man with reddish-blond hair, dressed in a grey, three-piece suit with a yellow handkerchief poking out of the breast pocket. He smiled and nodded at Mackinnon and Collins in turn.

"Oakland's," he said. "Finest quality at the best prices." He stuck out his hand. "Fred Oakland at your service."

Mackinnon shook his hand. "I'm afraid we're not shopping for furniture, sir."

Fred Oakland deflated like a popped balloon. "Are you sure? We have some really lovely new stock, excellent workmanship."

Mackinnon shook his head.

"Well, what do you want then?" Fred Oakland said peevishly, dropping his plummy vowels and slipping into a South London accent.

Mackinnon held out his warrant card, and Fred Oakland eyed it suspiciously, then said, "What do you want from me?"

"We're looking into the disappearance of a young woman."

"Oh." despite himself, Fred Oakland perked up, interested.

"She attended the academy next door," Mackinnon said. "Her name was Anya Blonski."

Fred Oakland frowned. "Never heard of her."

Collins fished around in his suit jacket for Anya's photograph. "Perhaps you knew her by sight."

Fred Oakland took the photograph of Anya and studied it. Henryk had brought that photograph to the Wood Street Police Station when he reported Anya missing. It was a good photo. A close-up shot of Anya from her chest upwards. Her fair hair was pushed back, giving a clear view of her pale face, and she was smiling at whoever had taken the photo.

Mackinnon hoped she was still smiling, wherever she was.

"I'm not sure," Fred Oakland said, frowning at the photo. "She looks vaguely familiar, but I'm not certain. Sorry." He handed the photograph back to Collins, who stared down at it for a moment before tucking it back in his pocket.

"That's all right," Mackinnon said. "Thanks for looking.

I suppose you don't have much to do with the Star Academy?"

"It's not really my cup of tea," Fred Oakland said. "I'm more into practical things." He gestured around the shop. "Carpentry, making things, that's my kind of art, not all that nonsense they get up to in those studios."

"You make this stuff yourself?" Collins asked, looking around

Fred Oakland shook his head. "Most of it's imported nowadays. It's more economical. I keep my hand in though. It's a family tradition. You should have seen some of the stuff my father made," he said, running his hand along the grain of a smooth oak table. "Now *he* was an artist."

"Did your father set up the business?" Mackinnon asked.

"We go back further than that. My great-grandfather started the business, and my grandfather bought this store. It's been in Oakland hands ever since. Although," he looked around sadly, "things aren't quite what they were."

Mackinnon looked down at one of the red sale stickers. "This recession's hit a lot of people."

Fred Oakland nodded. "People just aren't interested in proper furniture these days. They buy all that flat-packed rubbish from the big chain stores."

He shook his head. "When my father was alive, we owned the whole building. But with the downturn, I had to rent out half the building. I couldn't stay afloat otherwise."

"Are the Cleeves family with their Star Academy your only tenants?" Mackinnon asked.

Fred Oakland nodded. "Yes, thank God. I couldn't handle any more. They're bad enough."

"Bad in what way?"

"Oh, just wanting more space, renovations, that sort of thing. I suppose it could be worse."

"Now," Fred Oakland said, smiling, "Are you sure I can't interest you in a handmade piece of furniture from Oakland's?" His plummy vowels returned as he launched his sales pitch. "I've got an exquisite high-backed chair, with longer legs than usual. Perfect for someone of your height."

CHAPTER EIGHTEEN

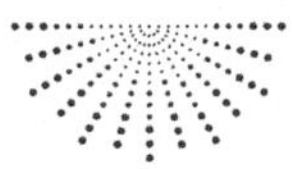

MACKINNON DIDN'T BUY THE chair, but he returned to Wood Street Station the proud owner of a new bookcase.

"Tell me the truth," Collins said. "You bought it because you felt sorry for him, didn't you?"

"It's very well made," Mackinnon said.

Collins shook his head. "Who would have thought it? You're a soft touch, Jack,"

"Yeah, yeah. Now back to the case in hand. We need to have a word with Henryk's last employer. Where did he work again? A pub?"

Collins grinned. "Yeah. A pub called The Old Griffin on the Shoreditch Road. Doesn't sound like the most salubrious establishment."

"Salubrious? That's a big word for you, Nick."

Collins pulled a face.

"How are we doing with that list of cruise ships?" Mackinnon asked.

"DC Webb is trawling through them now," Collins said. "The DI needs to authorise the checking of passenger lists as well as the staff ones. At the moment, we're relying on the good will of the cruise ship companies."

Mackinnon nodded. "We'll speak to him about it in the briefing. I'm pretty sure this whole case will be out of our hands soon."

Collins' head snapped up. "What do you mean?"

"DI Green will have to hand over the case to MIT eventually."

"What?" Collins' face glowed red. "He can't do that. Not now after we've been working on it. I know the details. He can't take me off it."

Collins must have seen the expression on Mackinnon's face. He turned away, then mumbled. "I mean, it's our case. We've worked the background."

"Yes, and we'll be able to brief MIT, thoroughly. We have to pass it on to the Major Investigation Team, Nick. It's murder."

Frustration clouded Collins' face for a moment, then he put his elbows on the desk and rested his head in his hands, clutching clumps of his short, fair hair in his fingers.

"Nick," Mackinnon said. "You do know there wasn't anything you could have done to stop this, don't you?"

Collins didn't look up, and when he spoke, his voice was quiet. "I rushed him. I just wanted to get home."

"It wouldn't have made a difference," Mackinnon said.

Collins pushed himself out of his chair. "Yeah, well, I'll have to live with the fact that I'll never know for sure."

CHAPTER NINETEEN

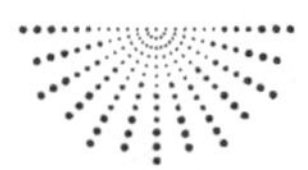

MACKINNON AND COLLINS WALKED along Shoreditch High Street.

"It's around here somewhere." Collins looked down at the map on his mobile phone. "We must be nearly there."

As they trudged past a Tesco Express store, Mackinnon took off his jacket and rolled up his shirtsleeves.

"That's it over there, isn't it? On the other side of the road." Mackinnon nodded at a modest pub called The Old Griffin. It was surrounded by scaffolding.

Collins frowned. "Doesn't look promising. Do you reckon it's open? Maybe they're renovating?"

"The door's open," Mackinnon said. "Let's take a look."

"It's a pub for locals, rather than tourists, that's for sure," Mackinnon said as they passed a market stall and started crossing the road.

The Old Griffin had a tired and grubby feel to it. The black and gold sign stuck high above the windows had faded over the years, and the windows were dark, dirty and impossible to see through.

"It's a girly pub." Collins said.

"Really? You've been before, have you?"

"No." Collins tapped his phone. "Googled it."

As they entered, the smell of stale beer flooded over them. Mackinnon blinked and took a quick look around, waiting for his eyes to adjust to the gloom. The pub was complete with wooden décor, tables and stools. The bar ran the length of the room. A pool table stood opposite the bar. Over by the far end of the room, near the toilets, was a small, elevated stage equipped with a chrome dancer's pole. Posters labelled 'Girls, Girls, Girls!' adorned the walls, offering free entrance before five pm and a fiver entrance fee afterwards.

Maybe they got busier later, but this afternoon, the place was dead. A lone drinker sat at the bar, staring down into his pint glass. A girl walked out of the ladies' toilets, wearing Perspex heels, and a spray-on, short, red dress. She smiled broadly at Mackinnon and Collins and began to totter over to them. How she managed to walk in those things was anyone's guess.

Mackinnon shook his head and held up his warrant card.

The effect was instantaneous. The woman's face soured. "What do you lot want?"

Her reaction wasn't really a surprise. The relationship between the police and workers in places like this wasn't exactly harmonious. Enforcing rules, and maintaining distance between the dancers and punters was just one of the many reasons for clashes over the years.

"Is the manager about?" Mackinnon asked.

She gave a surly nod, then click-clacked on her heels over to the bar.

"Brian," she yelled. "There's police out here."

A giant beast of a man entered the bar. He wore a tight t-shirt, and the underarms were stained with sweat. His hair was cropped close to his scalp.

He scratched his couple-of-days-old stubble.

"All right, can I help you?" he asked, his low rumbling voice sounding like the last thing he wanted to do was help them.

Mackinnon sensed Collins bristle with frustration beside him. He was spoiling for a bust-up. Nothing would make him happier right now than making an arrest.

Mackinnon walked up to the bar, determined to take charge of this one. Collins could simmer away, blaming himself. But Mackinnon couldn't let him mess this up.

"I hope so." Mackinnon said. He showed his warrant card to Brian.

Brian narrowed his eyes and studied it. "You're a bit out of your way, aren't you? We deal with the Met boys round here."

"What's your full name, please, sir?"

"Brian. Brian Mann. I'm the manager here." He wiped his hands on a towel, then leaned against the bar. "What's all this about?"

"I'm DS Mackinnon, and this is DC Collins. We want to talk to you about Henryk Blonski."

"Henryk? Yeah, he works here most nights. He's a good worker." Brian Mann crossed his arms, which caused his biceps to bulge and made his chest look twice as wide. "He's not in any trouble, is he?"

"Henryk Blonski was killed last night," Collins said.

"Killed?" Brian Mann repeated. His arms dropped down to his sides, and he looked deflated by the news. He stared down at the bar for a moment, then rubbed a hand over his stubbly chin. "How did it happen? Car accident?"

Mackinnon shook his head. "He was murdered."

"Murdered?" The big man shuddered, and his belly rippled under his tight t-shirt. "Why would anyone want to hurt Henryk? Was it a mugging? Poor bastard."

"We're investigating," Mackinnon said. "What can you tell us about Henryk? How long had he worked here?"

"How long? It would have been coming up to a year next month. He was a decent bloke. Trustworthy, you know?"

"How many shifts did he work a week?" The bar manager wiped a rag across the surface of the bar, a habit, something to do with his hands, rather than a conscious action.

"He worked from twelve 'til nine, five days a week. He took a few extra shifts here and there. He needed the money. He was always looking for overtime." Brian Mann's head snapped up as if he had just thought of something. "He was on the books. All legit. He paid his taxes."

Mackinnon nodded. "Its all right, Brian. We want to find out what happened to Henryk. We're not concerned about him working a few extra hours. Can you tell us if he had any trouble at work? Any customers getting too close to the girls? Anyone that might have been upset with Henryk?"

"No. He was a good bloke. Worked hard, but kept to

himself. I deal with the customers who step out of line. I make sure no one takes advantage of the girls. Henryk just worked the bar."

"Did you ever meet any of his friends?" Mackinnon asked. "Did he hang around with a certain crowd?"

"Not that I know of."

"Did he ever talk about his sister?"

"His sister? Yeah, he did. Anya. He thought the world of her. They shared a flat on the Towers Estate. I've got his address on file somewhere if you need it."

A flash of memory hit Mackinnon – an image of Henryk Blonski lying outside his own front door, blood pooled around his body.

"Thank you, but we have his address," Mackinnon said. "Do you know where he worked before he came here?" the bar manager nodded. "Yeah, he gave me references when he started. He was a dishwasher in a restaurant. I forget the name. I'll go and get his file for you. Take a seat. Want a drink while you wait?"

"No we're good, but thanks."

As they waited for Brian to come back with the file, Mackinnon looked around the pub. It was a serious, no frills place. The tables and chairs had seen better days. The dim lighting may have helped to hide some of the wear and tear, but it still looked cheap. The chrome bar the girls used for dancing had lost its shine, and greasy fingerprints smeared the surface.

Brian stomped back through the door into the bar.

He passed Mackinnon a couple of sheets of paper. "That's all I've got. It's not a lot to show for a man's life, is it?"

"No," Mackinnon said. "It isn't. Tell me, did you ever meet Anya, Henryk's sister?"

Brian looked amused. "God, no. Henryk would have been horrified at the thought of Anya coming here. I'm not saying he was a prude. I mean, he was nice to the girls working here, but he would never have let Anya anywhere near this place. He put her on a bit of a pedestal, I think."

Mackinnon nodded. "When was Henryk's last shift?"

"Tuesday, he knocked off at nine."

"Was that the last time you saw him?"

Brian's face crumpled. "Yeah, that was the last time. Poor bastard."

CHAPTER TWENTY

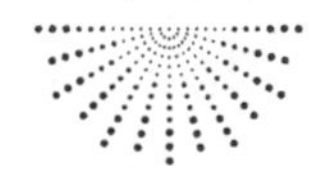

VICTORIA TRENT WAS WOKEN by something slamming into her shoulder. She opened her eyes, but it was pitch black. What was going on? Where was she?

Then she remembered. The house. The fake audition.

Panic bubbled up in her chest.

Why couldn't she straighten her legs? And what the hell was covering her mouth?

She could taste plastic and the chemical tang of adhesive. The bastard put tape over her mouth to silence her.

She screamed, but the sound was muffled by the gag and came out more like a high-pitched grunt. She couldn't breathe, couldn't suck enough oxygen through her nose. She felt her chest constrict. God, she recognised this feeling. She was going to have an asthma attack. She was going to die here.

She tried to breathe steadily through her nose, without panicking. She hadn't had an attack since she was a child. If she could just calm down and slow her breathing, she might be able to figure a way out of this mess.

At least, he hadn't bound her hands together, and she still had her clothes on. She put her hands up to her mouth and gently tugged the tape covering it. It didn't come away easily. As she pulled harder, it peeled away, millimetre-by-millimetre, and it felt like it took a few layers of skin with it.

Once the tape was off, she gulped down air, and gradually, the tight band of pain around her chest eased.

She reached her hands out, touching some kind of fabric. Her fingers scraped the surface. She was inside some sort of compartment. She was trapped.

A new kind of cold fear passed through Victoria. She felt light-headed and woozy, as if she might pass out. But she fought against it. She had to get a grip on herself.

She wrestled with the fabric wrapped around her and pushed upwards as hard as she could. It was only fabric; surely, she could rip it.

Her arms strained against the material until they ached from the effort. It wasn't working. There was no give in the material at all. She was caught like an animal in a trap.

She didn't understand why he had done this, or why he selected her, but she wasn't injured, and she would get away. The bastard picked the wrong person. She wasn't a victim. She would fight back with everything she had.

She needed to keep calm and think her way out of this. Her hands explored the small compartment. If only he'd left her bloody handbag, she could have phoned for help.

Victoria searched her memory, trying to work out what on earth he could want from her, but her mind felt sluggish and slow. He'd drugged her, injected her with something.

She'd have to play him, talk him round, tell him she wasn't angry, that if he'd just let her go, they could forget this ever happened. No one would need to know. She'd make him understand that this whole thing was crazy. How could he expect to get away with something like this? What he was doing was illegal, for Christ's sake. He could get locked up for years over this.

Then once he let her go, she'd head straight to the police and make sure they annihilated him.

"Let me out!" she screamed, struggling against the tough fabric.

There was no response. She started to pray, softly, "Please, get me out of this, God. I'll do anything if only…"

What was that noise?

Victoria's body tensed. She held her breath and listened. There was a slight ticking noise. A clock? No, faster than a clock. Then a point of dazzling light appeared above her. It was a zip! Someone was undoing a zip.

Her arms flew up towards the opening, struggling to get free. With her head and upper body free of the fabric, she sat there for a moment, blinking at the bright light.

She looked down, staring at the blue nylon material bunched up around her. Shit. He'd put her in a bloody sports bag. She stood quickly, trying to lift her legs out of the bag, but as she struggled, her legs wouldn't work properly. She felt like a newborn deer, staggering around on wobbly legs.

She fell to her knees, looking around for him. But he was gone. He'd left her alone in a room filled with a collection of strange equipment.

CHAPTER TWENTY-ONE

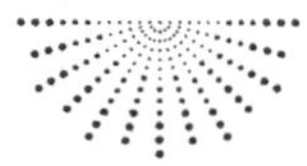

FIFTEEN MINUTES AFTER THEIR arrival back at Wood Street Station, Collins waved Mackinnon over to his desk.

"Come and have a look at this," Collins said, pointing at his computer screen.

Collins scooted his chair over, so Mackinnon could have an unobstructed view. Collins had opened up the YouTube website.

"I found a video of Nathan Cleeves' band, Vivid. Take a look at this. They're performing a song called 'You're Pretty Clever'."

As Collins pressed "play," a tinny, electronic beat started up, while on screen, five men dressed in black leather jackets and Lycra shorts bounded on stage, gyrating and strutting their stuff.

Mackinnon raised an eyebrow.

"It gets better," Collins said.

"I'm not sure I believe you."

Mackinnon was right to doubt Collins. It got worse. A lot worse.

When Collins finally muted the video, he looked up at Mackinnon. "What was it called? 'Pretty Clever'?" Collins grunted. "It's not clever, and it's certainly not pretty."

It's not what I call music, either," Mackinnon said. "Did he really get six Brit Awards for that?"

Collins nodded. "I'm afraid so."

Still puzzling over how anybody could describe Vivid's performance as a work of art, Mackinnon and Collins headed to DI Green's office for another briefing.

They were using the DI's office, as the briefing rooms were full. The finance unit were working on a high-profile fraud case, and MIT had commandeered the others.

It didn't really matter as the four of them fitted in the DI's office without a problem: DC Webb, Collins, Mackinnon and DI Green.

DI Green was already talking things through with DC Webb, when Mackinnon and Collins entered and pulled up chairs, muttering quick apologies for arriving late.

"As I was saying," DI Green said, looking pointedly at Mackinnon and Collins. "The hostage situation is ongoing, and MIT is up to its neck right now. I will be handing over to DCI Brookbank–"

"If they're so busy, why don't we continue to work the Blonski case?" Collins asked. His knee was bouncing up and down like a nervous tic.

"Murder always goes to the Major Investigation Team," DI Green said and set his lips in a firm line, signalling an end to the discussion.

But Collins didn't pick up on that, or if he did, he was determined to ignore it.

"But it's our case. We found him. We–"

"No," DI Green said. "Your case is the disappearance of Anya Blonski, not Henryk Blonski's murder." His voice had a steely edge.

Collins charged on, oblivious. "But I found his body."

DI Green shot Collins a withering look. "DC Collins, if you feel you are becoming too emotionally attached to this case, I could remove you from the Anya Blonski investigation as well."

Collins fell silent.

"I need my officers to be cool-headed and logical, is that clear?"

Collins responded with a curt nod.

This case was clearly eating away at him. Mackinnon spoke up, trying to ease the pressure on Collins.

"When will we brief MIT, sir?"

DI Green glanced at his watch. "Soon. I hoped DI Hussein would be here by now." He shrugged. "While we wait, tell me where we stand at the moment."

"We looked into Anya's movements on Tuesday, the day of her disappearance," Mackinnon said. "She worked her usual shift at Starbucks in the morning and took her normal class at the Star Academy in the afternoon. Everyone we spoke to at the academy told us Anya left town to work on a cruise ship. But no one actually heard that from Anya herself. And no one remembers who originally mentioned the cruise ship."

"Have we located Anya's parents yet?"

"They're in Poland," Mackinnon said. "DC Collins got

their telephone number from the address book found at the Blonski's flat, and the *Policja* contacted the parents and broke the news."

"Right. So we have no sightings of Anya Blonksi since Tuesday?" DI Green asked. "What do you think? Did she just run off, or do you think something's happened to her?"

Collins spoke up. "No one matching Anya Blonski's description was admitted to any of the local hospitals. None of the cruise companies have any records of an employee named Anya Blonksi."

There was a knock at the door, and DI Hussein from MIT poked his head in the room. "Sorry I'm late. DCI Brookbank sends his apologies."

"Ah, DI Hussein. We were just discussing the Blonski case. Have a seat."

DI Hussein pulled a face. "I'm really sorry, but I can't stay. The DCI sent me down here to ask if you could give him the file and send one of your officers over at six to attend the MIT briefing."

DI Green frowned. "Oh, I see. I understand you're busy, but–"

"We're snowed under. All hell's kicking off at the Towers Estate."

DI Green's shoulders slumped. "Oh, all right then. DC Collins will go to the MIT briefing at six, and we'll keep looking into Anya Blonski's disappearance. It could have something to do with her brother's murder."

"Fantastic," DI Hussein said, already backing out of the room. "Appreciate your help. See you later, Collins."

After DI Hussein left the room, DI Green sighed heavily.

"So much for MIT," Collins muttered under his breath.

"Right, where were we?" DI Green asked.

"We talked to Anya's colleagues at Starbucks and the owners of the academy Anya attended."

"Nathan Cleeves is at the top of my list," Collins said. "He is a thirty-nine-year-old ex-boy-band member and an arrogant, little toe rag."

"Is there any reason he tops your list?" DI Green asked. "Other than the fact he is an arrogant toe rag, of course."

"He's got previous," Collins said. "Attacking paparazzi outside a nightclub in 2002, and my instinct tells me he's hiding something."

DI Green frowned. "Mackinnon? What do you make of him?"

Mackinnon understood where Collins was coming from. Nathan Cleeves gave a very bad first impression, and Mackinnon didn't like him any more than Collins did. But instincts weren't enough. They needed to work with the facts, process the evidence step-by-step, then move onto the theories.

"Nathan Cleeves was obnoxious and sullen. The last thing he wanted to do was help us with our enquiries." Mackinnon leaned forward, "But we don't have any evidence to suggest he knows where Anya is. He told us as far as he was concerned, she'd gone off on a cruise ship."

"You can't deny he looked shifty though," Collins said.

"All right, shiftiness aside, is there anyone else who rang alarm bells?" DI Green asked.

"Jim Meadows," Mackinnon said. "He worked at Starbucks with Anya. He definitely had a crush on her, but I don't think there was anything more to it."

"What about customers?" DI Green asked "A pretty girl

like that, there's bound to have been a couple sniffing around."

"Nothing ominous, according to Jim Meadows. No boyfriend either."

DI Green sniffed and shuffled a few sheets of paper on his desk.

"I find that hard to believe." DI Green held up the six-by-nine-inch photo of Anya that Henryk gave Collins when he first reported her missing. "Ask around again. Dig deeper, there has to be someone. And, Collins, pay Nathan Cleeves another visit. Let him know we're watching him."

Collins nodded. "That will be a pleasure."

DI Green sighed and leaned back in his chair. He linked his fingers together and rested his hands on his stomach. "I'm going to have to speak to the super about staffing. I know MIT are under a lot of pressure, but we can't handle Henryk Blonski's murder. It doesn't fall under our remit."

DI Green reached for the telephone on his desk, signalling the end of their meeting.

Mackinnon got to his feet, thinking about Henryk Blonski and wondering how he would have felt about falling outside some bureaucratic remit.

"One more thing, sir," Mackinnon said. "We found Anya's passport at the flat she shared with Henryk. We've checked, and she hasn't applied for another one. It doesn't look good."

"No," DI Green said, gripping the telephone handset to his ear. "No, it doesn't."

CHAPTER TWENTY-TWO

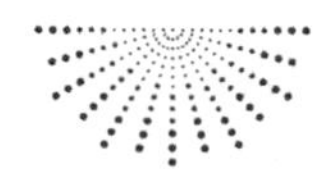

VICTORIA TRENT REMAINED CROUCHED on the floor as she slowly looked around the room. Where the hell was she? It wasn't anywhere she'd been before. She was sure of that. It suddenly struck her that she couldn't hear anything. No traffic, no voices and no footsteps. Only silence.

As someone who lived in London all her life, Victoria wasn't used to it being so quiet. Where had he taken her?

She could hear nothing but her own heartbeat, thumping too fast, and her raw, rasping breath. She tried to calm down. Remembering her old counselling sessions, she tried to find her safe place, but there was no calm, no inner peace. Only panic.

She didn't even know if it was day or night. There were no windows in the room. An ugly, bare bulb that flickered as if it might go out at any moment was the only source of light.

There was a bad smell hanging in the air, a stinking blend of body odour and public toilets.

On the floor in front of her was a bottle of mineral water. Her mouth felt dry and sour. She must have been unconscious for a while. She grabbed the water and guzzled it down greedily.

The room was arranged like a stage set. To her right, she saw cameras, three of them, mounted on tripods. They looked professional, like something you'd see on the set of a TV studio. Held up at various positions around the room were huge lights on stands. They weren't switched on. Beside one of the lights was a fuzzy ball of grey fur on a stick – a sound boom. All this stuff was set up for recording.

Victoria felt a new stab of panic. What was he going to record? What was he going to do to her?

Did he make some kind of sex videos?

She had to get out of here. She flung herself at the door and yanked the handle. It was locked, so she pounded on the door with her fists.

"Let me out! Let me out of here, now!"

The door was covered with some kind of fabric-covered panels.

She heard a movement, a scraping, and turned around, pressing her back against the door. *Oh God, he was in the room.* Victoria's eyes scoured the dark corners. Where was he hiding?

"It's no good," a voice said. "The room is soundproofed."

Victoria's knees buckled, and she sank to the floor.

It wasn't him.

The voice belonged to a woman.

CHAPTER TWENTY-THREE

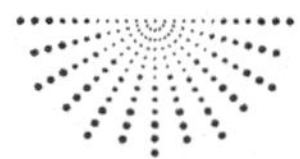

AFTER THE BRIEFING WITH DI Green, Collins sat at his desk, scowling as he sorted through the file on Henryk Blonski, ready to hand over the details to MIT.

Like Collins, Mackinnon didn't want to hand the case to anyone else. It felt like defeat, like admitting they didn't try hard enough.

Mackinnon peeled back the plastic cover of his cheese sandwich. It was all they had left at the canteen, and the cheese looked more plastic than the cover.

He'd just taken his first bite, when his mobile rang. Typical. He put the sandwich on his desk and reached into his pocket for his phone. The ring tone sounded very much like Queen's "Don't Stop Me Now."

Bloody DC Webb.

He was always messing about with people's phones. It wasn't even safe to leave your phone unguarded in a police station with him around. Still, with the Queen ring tone, he supposed he had gotten off lightly, compared to Collins last month. Webb had changed the text language on Collins mobile to Arabic. And changing it back was no simple matter when all the phone menus were in a language you couldn't understand.

And at least DC Webb changed the ring tone to a song he liked.

Mackinnon glanced at the screen. A London number he didn't recognise flashed on the display.

"DS Mackinnon."

"This is Rachel Cleeves, Detective. I spoke to you this morning. I suppose it is all right to call you on this number, is it? It was on the card you left with my father."

"It's fine," Mackinnon said. "What can I do to help?"

"It's one of my students. She hasn't shown up to class." Rachel said the words in a rush as though she'd been holding them in for a while and was relieved to finally say them.

The back of Mackinnon's neck tingled. This didn't feel good at all.

"What's the student's name?" Mackinnon asked.

"God, I'm being an idiot," Rachel said. "I'm paranoid, I guess. Your visit this morning made me jump to conclusions. It's probably nothing, but she isn't answering her phone either. I'm sorry." Rachel's voice sounded really scared.

"Not at all," Mackinnon said. "I can drop by in say thirty minutes, and you can give me the details."

"No!" Mackinnon heard Rachel's sharp intake of breath.

"I mean it's not a good idea. My mother would kill me if she knew I'd been talking to you. She thinks it's bad for business. I'll meet you somewhere. Do you know ZiZi's? It's just around the corner from the academy."

"Sure. I'll meet you there."

After Mackinnon hung up, he sat at his desk for a moment, staring at the phone. This morning Rachel Cleeves seemed cold and standoffish. The very last person Mackinnon would have expected to volunteer information. What had changed? Was it genuine concern for her student?

Part of being a detective required him to constantly question everyone's motivation. Mackinnon never gave anyone the benefit of the doubt. All actions had a sinister motive until proven otherwise. That was a good thing at work. A great thing even. Outside work, it became hard to switch that reasoning off. And more and more these days, Mackinnon found himself doubting everyone.

Maybe Rachel Cleeves was genuinely upset, or perhaps she had an ulterior motive. There was only one way to find out.

Mackinnon picked up his mobile and headed out.

The lunch trade at ZiZi's had already died away, so he spotted Rachel Cleeves easily. She sat inside the restaurant at one of the wooden tables. She hadn't taken off her cardigan, despite the warm weather. She had a cup of coffee in front of her, which she stirred constantly. She looked tense, agitated.

Mackinnon took off his grey suit jacket and hung it on the chair opposite Rachel Cleeves. "Hello," he said as he sat down.

"Victoria Trent," Rachel Cleeves said and dropped her spoon so it clattered against the side of the cup. She swallowed. "That's her name, Victoria. She's never missed a class before."

Rachel bit down on her bottom lip, and Mackinnon noticed she'd applied lipstick. Her cheeks looked flushed too. In a way that was too uniform to be natural. Why had she dolled herself up?

He was sure she hadn't been wearing makeup earlier.

"Of course, she might just have a touch of flu or something," Rachel Cleeves put her cold fingers on top of Mackinnon's hand. "Do you think I'm over reacting?"

Mackinnon leaned back from the table and pulled his hand away gently.

"It's better to be safe than sorry," Mackinnon said. "Can you give me any more details?"

Mackinnon waved to a waiter, ordered a black coffee, then listened to Rachel Cleeves as she described Victoria Trent. Rachel passed him a slip of paper. As Mackinnon looked down at the address written in scratchy, small handwriting, he asked, "Does she have a boyfriend?"

"Not that I know of." Rachel Cleeves shook her head. "I'm being silly, aren't I? It's just that when I rang her mobile, I got a message telling me it's switched off, and after all your questions about Anya..."

"I'm glad you told me," Mackinnon said.

"Really?"

For the first time, she gave a genuine smile, and her face lit up. She was actually quite attractive when she smiled.

Mackinnon nodded. "I'll pop round there now and check it out."

CHAPTER TWENTY-FOUR

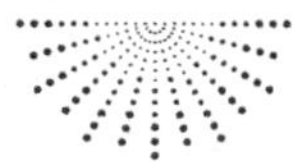

THE ADDRESS RACHEL CLEEVES gave him for Victoria Trent was on the Towers Estate, not far from Jubilee House. Victoria and Anya were practically neighbours. Was that the connection? Was the Star Academy a red herring?

Mackinnon arrived on the Towers Estate just after four. It was a warm day, and the local kids were playing on the streets with water pistols. Not the small, dribbly little things Mackinnon played with when he was a kid. These were brightly coloured, pump-action monsters. The kids looked like they were having great fun. Mackinnon watched as they darted along the pavement, their parents nowhere to be seen.

"Watch yourselves, lads," he said as the smaller of the two boys barrelled into him in his desperate attempt to escape the spray from his friend's gun.

Seeing as they were on the Towers Estate, he expected a mouthful of abuse, or a face-full of water in response, but the little boy just grinned up at him, showing off the gap in his front teeth. "Sorry," he said before charging off down the pavement in pursuit of his friend.

Mackinnon watched him go and smiled. Those water pistols did look like fun. He wondered, briefly, if Chloe's daughters would like them, then dismissed it. They were too old for that. Shame, Mackinnon wouldn't have minded trying one out himself.

He headed on past Jubilee House. The crime scene had already been processed. And there was no sign that poor Henryk Blonski lost his life here just two days ago. Mackinnon put his hands in his pockets and walked faster. He didn't want to linger.

Burgess House, where Victoria Trent lived, was a newer building than Jubilee House. Grey concrete, instead of red brick, and at least five storeys taller.

According to the address Rachel Cleeves gave him, Victoria Trent lived on the third floor. Grateful he didn't have to take the lift, Mackinnon headed for the stairwell. It smelled of bleach, but underneath the chlorine, the stench of rubbish lingered.

Mackinnon took shallow breaths as he climbed the stairs and thought about Chloe's daughters. He couldn't get them water pistols. He knew enough about teenage girls to realise that was a bad idea. Unfortunately, he didn't know enough to imagine what would be a good idea. A gift might help get them onside. But it might seem as if he were trying to buy their affection.

Mackinnon reached the third floor and exited the stairwell into the lobby. He glanced down at the piece of paper in his hand. Number thirty-one.

Straightaway, Mackinnon noticed Victoria Trent's mail wasn't pushed completely through the letterbox. That meant she hadn't been able to collect her post.

Mackinnon rang the doorbell and listened. He heard the cheerful jingle and waited. After a few moments, there was still no response, so he rapped on the door with his knuckles and called out Victoria's name, identifying himself as police.

Still no answer.

Mackinnon crouched down near the letterbox and put his face close to the opening. After a moment's hesitation, he took a deep breath through his nose.

Then he sighed with relief. No smell of decay. He stood straight and raised his fist to knock one last time.

Then he froze.

He just remembered what Belinda Cleeves had said this morning. One little word that made a world of difference. She said, "*They*."

She said, "*They* go off to the cruise ships."

Mackinnon fumbled for his phone, and Collins answered on the second ring.

"Jesus, Nick," Mackinnon said. "I don't think Anya Blonski was the first Star Academy girl to go missing."

CHAPTER TWENTY-FIVE

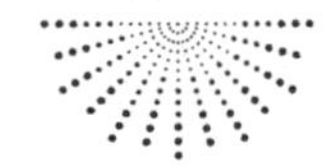

IT TOOK A MOMENT for Collins to process what Mackinnon was driving at.

"I was thinking back to our conversation with Belinda Cleeves," Mackinnon said, "And I remembered that she said, 'they'."

"What?"

"She said *they* go to the cruise ships."

"Yeah, rather than work at their craft. So?"

"*They* as in plural, Nick. *They* as in more than one girl have left the Star Academy under similar circumstances."

"Yeah, but you don't think…? I mean, girls must leave of their own accord all the time."

"Maybe, but I want to be sure."

Mackinnon told Collins he would go back to the academy and get a list of all the girls who left for the cruise ships. He was probably overanalysing this, seeing evil possibilities that might not be real. Maybe. But in his opinion, it was better to be cautious.

"I'll speak to Rachel Cleeves," Mackinnon said, pulling a hand over his ear to block out the noise of a bus accelerating away from the curb.

"Oh, yes," Collins said. "Reckon she'd be keen to get some one-on-one time with you." Collins' dirty laugh echoed through the phone. Mackinnon imagined Collins winking as he spoke.

"I just meant she seemed more helpful than the rest of the Cleeves family. More willing to talk."

"You're probably right," Collins said "I reckon she fancies you. So she'd be more likely to hand over the names."

"No." Mackinnon said. "It's because she's worried about the missing girls, not because she fancies me."

"Oh, yeah. Well, why didn't she ring me then? I gave her my card."

"You sound almost jealous, Nick."

"What?" Collins snorted "Don't be ridiculous. I'm married and I–"

"I've got to get on. You can tell me all about your theories when I get back to the station with the list." Mackinnon hung up without waiting for a reply.

"You shouldn't have drunk that water," the female voice said.

Victoria inched towards the familiar voice. It was coming from a corner of the room deep in shadow.

"Anya?"

There was a pause.

"Yes." Anya crawled forward, and Victoria shrank back away from her.

Anya's face was bruised and bloody. On her shoulder, there was a large, angry, red mark, which looked like a burn.

"What happened to your arm?" Victoria asked.

Victoria followed Anya's gaze. She stared at the long metal contraption, with a forked end, propped up against the wall.

"What's that?" Victoria asked, even though she didn't really want to hear the answer.

"A cattle prod. He uses it if we don't want to take part in his games."

Victoria shivered and noticed Anya's hands were tied together with blue, nylon rope. "I'll untie you. We'll get out of here, together. There's two of us now," she said, forcing her voice to sound confident.

"There were two of us before," Anya muttered.

"What did you say?"

"Nothing. It doesn't matter."

They were silent for a few moments, then Anya frowned and nodded at Victoria's forearm. "What happened? Did he do that to you?"

Victoria fought the impulse to cover herself. What did it matter now anyway? She looked down at the small, circular, red marks on her arm.

"No, he didn't. They're old scars."

Scars from another lifetime, Victoria thought. She closed her eyes and saw her stepfather closing in on her, a cigarette in his hand, a twisted grin on his mouth. She would never forget the look of pleasure in his eyes as he pressed the glowing end onto her smooth, eight-year-old skin for the first time.

She pulled her arm away from Anya gently and tugged down her sleeve. She couldn't think about that now. She needed to concentrate on finding a way out of this situation.

"Henryk is looking for you," Victoria said and saw hope flare briefly in Anya's eyes. "He's spoken to the police, told them you're missing. It won't be long before they find us."

Anya squeezed her eyes shut. "Henryk…" A small, solitary tear wound its way down her cheek.

"He came to see me," Victoria said. "He was really worried. He knew something was wrong." Victoria squeezed Anya's hand. "Your brother is a good man."

Anya began to cry, and Victoria hugged her tightly.

"It's all right. They'll find us," Victoria whispered.

But that only made Anya sob harder.

Victoria was starting to feel dizzy. "I don't feel well."

Her head felt as if it were stuffed with cotton wool.

"It's the water," Anya said. "He drugs it. But sometimes, it is better to sleep."

No! Victoria didn't want to sleep. She had to stay awake and keep her wits sharp.

She reached for the blue, nylon rope looped around Anya's wrists. "I'll untie you. When he comes back, we can make a run for it."

Anya yanked her hands away. "Don't bother. He'll only re-tie the rope and make it tighter next time. Anyway, you won't be able to run anywhere. You'll be asleep soon."

Victoria shook her head, but she couldn't reply. Her

tongue felt too thick, and she didn't have the energy to form the right words. Why didn't Anya want to help plan their escape?

Victoria swallowed. She felt nauseous and groggy. She leaned over and rested her head on Anya's lap.

She felt the muscles in Anya's legs tense at the contact, but Victoria was too tired to care.

CHAPTER TWENTY-SIX

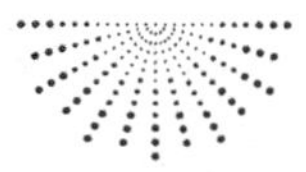

WHEN MACKINNON ARRIVED BACK at the Star Academy, the same receptionist, Pippa Adams, sat at the desk. She had clearly finished filing her nails ages ago. Now, she painted them, carefully stroking the tiny brush along each one, leaving them a shiny burgundy.

"I hope I'm not interrupting," Mackinnon said.

"Oh!" the receptionist's head snapped up, and her hand jumped, smearing polish along the entire length of her index finger. "Damn." She wiped away the excess polish with a tissue, then smiled apologetically at Mackinnon.

"I'm sorry," she said, flapping her hands about like a bird with wounded wings. "How can I help?"

"I'd like to speak to Rachel Cleeves, please. Could you call her and tell her I'm here?"

The receptionist picked up the telephone handset gingerly, careful not to smudge her polish.

Less than a minute later, Rachel came clattering down

the stairs. Her mousy hair had escaped from her French plait, and her eyes were wide open.

"What are you doing here?" she asked in a horrified whisper.

"I need to ask a favour," Mackinnon said.

"Not here," Rachel said and started to push Mackinnon to the door. "Outside."

Mackinnon was a foot taller and several stone heavier than Rachel Cleeves, and at first, he stood his ground, irritated by her reaction. Then he spotted the receptionist eyeing them curiously, saw Rachel's desperate look at the CCTV camera above the reception desk, and thought it might be a good idea to talk to her without an audience.

As they stepped outside, into the warmth of the afternoon, Rachel Cleeves turned on Mackinnon, furious. "What were you thinking? I told you not to come here, my mother will be livid."

Mackinnon stared at her for a moment, stunned. She really was terrified of Belinda Cleeves. At thirty-five-years-old, Rachel Cleeves lived and worked with her family. Would she ever manage to escape her domineering mother?

"I need your help, Rachel," Mackinnon said. "When I spoke to your mother this morning, she mentioned other girls who left the Star Academy to work on the cruise ships."

Rachel shrugged, then glanced back to the academy entrance to make sure she wasn't being watched.

"Have other girls left the academy recently?" Mackinnon asked.

Rachel shrugged. "Some, I guess."

"I'll need a list of names and contact details of those students. Can you get that for me?"

Rachel's eyes opened wide, then she blinked rapidly. "Why? Do you think..." She shook her head. "No, I can't. I don't know how to get the files. I don't have access to the students' records."

"It's important," Mackinnon said. "I hope nothing has happened to these girls, but I have to make sure."

"No, no," Rachel said, backing away. "I shouldn't even have mentioned Victoria. I was just being stupid. Just forget it, please."

"Ah, Detective Mackinnon, isn't it?" A female voice asked.

Mackinnon turned. Belinda Cleeves stood behind him with her back to the setting sun, so she appeared as a silhouette, and Mackinnon couldn't see her face clearly to judge her expression.

He heard Rachel gasp.

"Rachel, invite the detective inside. It's vulgar to stand around talking on street corners," Belinda Cleeves said.

Rachel gave a little bob of her head. "Yes, Mother."

The three of them stepped back inside the cool reception. Belinda Cleeves turned to the receptionist, who was watching them eagerly. "Go and get yourself a cup of tea, Pippa, dear."

"That's all right, Madame Cleeves. I've only just had one."

Belinda Cleeves glared at the girl until she scurried away.

"Now, Detective," Belinda Cleeves said, turning to Mackinnon, "what can we do to help?"

Rachel stared miserably at the floor.

Mackinnon had wanted to get the list of names from Rachel because he thought that would be the quickest and easiest way to get the information. Belinda Cleeves could cause trouble. He didn't think she'd hand over any information willingly.

He hoped by asking Rachel, he could get the names without having to wait around for a warrant. Paperwork slowed things down. And right now, with two missing girls, possibly more, time was something he lacked.

But now Belinda Cleeves stood in front of him, her tiny body tense, and a furious scowl on her face. He didn't have much choice.

"I'd like a list of all the students who left your Star Academy to work on cruise ships."

"Whatever for?" Belinda Cleeves asked, frowning.

"You mentioned other girls left before Anya, to work on cruise liners."

"Yes, it's quite common, I'm afraid, but why do you need a list?"

"Process of elimination," Mackinnon said

Belinda Cleeves eyed him suspiciously. "All right I'll see what I can do. Give me an hour and I'll email it to you."

"I don't mind waiting," Mackinnon said.

"I'm sure you have more important things to do, Detective. If you give me your email address, I'll email the list to you in an hour."

Mackinnon handed over another business card. He was on the verge of telling Belinda Cleeves he left his card with her husband this morning but remembered Rachel had probably taken it before she called him. So he handed

Belinda Cleeves a new card and kept his mouth shut. He didn't want to add to Rachel's troubles. It was better for Rachel if her mother didn't know she'd told Mackinnon about Victoria Trent.

Belinda Cleeves accepted Mackinnon's card with a perfunctory nod and turned to her daughter. "Come along, Rachel. You have a class starting in five minutes."

Rachel glanced back at Mackinnon as she was whisked along by her mother. Her eyes looked sad underneath her lowered lashes.

Mackinnon didn't understand. If she were that miserable, why didn't she just leave?

CHAPTER TWENTY-SEVEN

WITH AN HOUR TO kill before he could get his hands on the list Belinda Cleeves promised him, Mackinnon decided to pay a house visit and check out Nathan's alibi.

Mackinnon caught the DLR from Bank to Limehouse, then walked the short distance to Salmon Lane.

Anita Simeon lived in a three-storey townhouse. Mackinnon paused outside. Collins had said she was a dancer, but she had to be a pretty successful one if she could afford a place like this. Mackinnon rang the doorbell and waited.

The door opened, and a young girl with big, brown eyes stared out at him. He guessed she was about fifteen.

"I'm looking for Anita Simeon. My name's DS Mackinnon." He held out his warrant card.

The girl's eyes opened wide, and she raised a hand to her mouth. "That's me. What's wrong? Has there been an accident?"

Mackinnon shook his head. "No, nothing like that. I just want to ask you a few questions."

"I suppose you'd better come inside," Anita said, stepping back into the hallway to let Mackinnon in.

Mackinnon's immediate impression was the house had to belong to someone older than Anita. The frilly lace over the hall table, the fussy wallpaper and watercolours lined up on the wall all reflected an older person's tastes.

"Come through," Anita said, leading the way into the front room.

"Sorry, if I seem jumpy. I just thought the worst when you said you were a policeman. I thought something had happened to my mum and dad."

"Do you live with your parents?" Mackinnon asked.

Anita nodded.

Mackinnon paused for a moment, then said, "How old are you, Anita?"

"I'm seventeen."

The surprise must have registered on Mackinnon's face because she said, "Oh, I know I look younger. I get people saying that to me all the time." She shrugged.

"Do you know a man called Nathan Cleeves?" Mackinnon asked.

"Nathan?" Her eyes narrowed, and her body tensed. She was suddenly wary. "Yes, I know Nathan." She plucked at the sleeve of her fluffy, pink jumper. "Why? Is he in trouble?"

"No," Mackinnon said. "It's just a routine enquiry. Did you see him on Wednesday?"

"Wednesday?" Anita repeated, staring down at her

pink, oversized slippers. "Yes, I did see him on Wednesday night." Anita cradled her wrist in one hand and winced.

"Have you hurt yourself?" Mackinnon asked.

"Not really. I sprained it."

"Can you tell me what time you saw Nathan on Wednesday evening?"

"Um…" Anita chewed her lower lip before answering. "He arrived here around eight thirty, and we watched a couple of DVDs in my room."

Mackinnon nodded. "And what time did he leave?"

"Well…" Anita shot an anxious look at the door. "It's… well, you see… my parents don't know. You won't tell them, will you?"

Mackinnon shook his head.

Anita took a deep breath, then said, "He pretended to go home at ten, but I let him in the back door again just a few minutes later. My parents don't like him spending the night, you see."

"I see, so Nathan stayed the night with you?"

Anita nodded. "My parents will kill me if they find out."

Mackinnon sympathised with her parents. Nathan Cleeves was almost forty, and he was sneaking into a house to sleep with a girl barely past the age of consent. It made Mackinnon's skin crawl.

"Is that it, then?" Anita asked and looked at her watch. "Only, my parents will be home soon, and they'll jump to the wrong conclusion."

Mackinnon stood up. "Thanks for your help, Anita. I appreciate it."

He held out his hand, and as Anita reached to shake it,

the sleeve of her jumper moved, revealing a purple, circular bruise on her forearm.

"That looks painful," Mackinnon said.

"Oh, it's nothing," Anita said, pulling down her sleeve.

It didn't look like nothing. It looked as if someone had gripped her arm so tightly they'd left behind a finger-shaped bruise. It looked like abuse.

Mackinnon left the house, fuming. More determined than ever to find something on Nathan Cleeves.

CHAPTER TWENTY-EIGHT

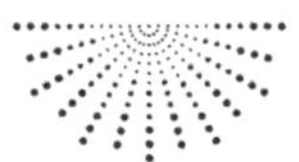

MACKINNON WALKED INTO WOOD Street Station, scrolling through the emails on his phone. It had been over an hour since he'd spoken to Belinda Cleeves, and there was still no sign of the e-mail she promised to send.

As he walked into the open plan offices on the second floor, the heat of the room hit him. He flung his jacket over a chair and stood beside Collins' desk. "Any news?"

Collins shook his head.

"Maybe I should ring her," Mackinnon said. "Maybe she typed the e-mail address in wrong?"

"I think she's probably doing it on purpose," Collins said. "She wants us to know she's in charge."

Mackinnon pulled over a chair and slumped down into it.

"In that case, I'll speak to the DI about getting a warrant," Mackinnon said. "We don't have time for her attitude."

Mackinnon rubbed a hand over his face, then circled his neck, trying to ease the stiffness. He felt weary to the bone.

"I need a coffee," Mackinnon said. "If that e-mail doesn't arrive by the time I get back, I'll start the paperwork for the warrant."

Collins nodded as Mackinnon got to his feet.

"Do you want a coffee?" Mackinnon asked.

Collins pointed to his half-empty cup on the desk. "I've still got one, thanks. How did it go at Anita Simeon's? Did she confirm Nathan's alibi?"

"She confirmed Nathan Cleeves is a scumbag."

Collins raised an eyebrow. "I already knew that."

"All right then, she confirmed he's even more of a scumbag than we originally thought. She's seventeen, Nick. Seventeen. She looks young for her age too."

"Seventeen?" Collins stared at Mackinnon. "But he's…" Collins rummaged through the paperwork on his desk, found the piece of paper he was looking for and stabbed at it with his finger. "He's practically forty."

"Creepy, isn't it? But she did confirm his alibi. She told me he snuck back into the house after her parents went to bed."

Collins' upper lip curved with disgust.

"That's not all. She had a bruise on her wrist, like someone had grabbed her." Mackinnon encircled his wrist with his fingers, remembering the pink and purple marks on Anita Simeon's arm.

"Bastard," Collins said.

"I don't know if it was Nathan who hurt her. She didn't want to talk to me about it."

"I bet it was." Collins said. He leaned forward, put his

elbows on the desk, then rested his head in his hands. "Why didn't I listen to Henryk Blonksi on Tuesday morning?"

"You did."

"I didn't pay enough attention."

Mackinnon put a hand on Collins' shoulder. "Don't beat yourself up about it. You couldn't have predicted what happened to Henryk Blonski. No one could."

"I spoke to Brookbank earlier, and he said the same thing."

"Brookbank?"

"The DCI in charge of MIT."

Mackinnon nodded. "I've heard of him. Have they got anything new on the Blonski murder?"

"Bits and pieces. They're looking into a couple of shady characters, who worked with Blonski when he first arrived in the UK. At the moment, they don't have any evidence to suggest that Henryk's death is linked to his sister's disappearance."

"Big coincidence."

"Brookbank said he's keeping an open mind, but MIT are looking into the possibility he might have been a pimp."

Mackinnon frowned. That didn't fit with what Mackinnon knew about Henryk Blonski. But MIT were working the case now, so perhaps they'd uncovered more information. Maybe Henryk Blonski wasn't as much of an upright citizen as he first thought.

"I've never spoken to Brookbank before; what's he like?" Mackinnon asked.

Mackinnon was keen to move to the Major Investigation Team, but he'd heard Brookbank often described as a hard task master.

Collins paused for a moment before answering. "He's certainly a personality. A bit domineering perhaps, but he's probably very nice, once you get to know him." Collins looked around the office and seemed relieved when no one seemed to be paying attention to their conversation.

He left Collins to his paperwork and went in search of coffee.

On his return, he noticed Collins hunched over the front of his computer monitor. His face was drained of colour.

Mackinnon put his coffee cup down on his desk and walked over to Collins. "What is it, Nick? Did she send the email?"

Collins looked up, and something in his eyes made Mackinnon's stomach plummet to his shoes.

"Jesus, Jack" Collins said. "There's eight of them. Eight girls."

* * *

They took the news straight to DI Green. Mackinnon watched the detective inspector's face tense as he read the names on the list.

"Have all these girls been reported missing by their families?" DI Green asked, his voice hoarse.

"Seven of the girls are on the missing persons list, sir," Collins said.

"Seven girls. Shit." DI Green picked up the phone, waited a moment, then spoke into the handset. "I need to speak to Superintendent Wright … as soon as possible … Yes, it's very urgent."

DI Green replaced the receiver and chewed on his

bottom lip. Then, as if he'd just remembered Mackinnon and Collins were in the room with him, he looked up.

"We're going to need extra bodies on this. Staff shortages or not, we can't handle this on our own." He swallowed. "Okay, first things first. Collins, you speak to DCI Brookbank and let MIT know about this development. Then I want you to double-check those names against the misper list again – check next of kin contact details. We're going to need–"

"We do have contact details for next of kin," Collins said. "Belinda Cleeves sent them over with the names. I'm not sure if they are up to date, but–"

"Okay, good. We have to contact their families. We need to know if these girls have shown up and are only still on the list because no one bothered to inform us. We'll look bloody stupid if these girls are at home, safely tucked up in bed."

DI Green paused, biting down on his lip again. "And for God's sake, when you speak to the families, just tell them it's a routine, missing person follow-up. We don't want to trigger mass panic."

DI Green rubbed a hand over his creased brow. "We can't miss anything. If these girls are missing, we'll need to check bank accounts, phone records…" He shook his head. "I hope to God this is a false alarm."

DI Green's phone rang, and he snatched it up, nodding once before saying, "I'll be right there."

DI Green stood up. "I'm going to see the super now. You know what to do?"

"Sir," Mackinnon said. "I was going to pay a visit to Victoria Trent's parents. They live in Bethnal Green. She's only just gone missing, so the details should be fresher for her parents. They might remember more than the others. They might remember a new friend she made, or some detail about the Star Academy… Help us narrow it down."

"I know who it is," Collins said. "Nathan Cleeves."

"We don't know that, Collins," DI Green said. "We have to pursue every line of enquiry. Jack, visit Victoria Trent's parents, then get back here as soon as you can, all right? I'll set up a time for a briefing tonight."

Mackinnon nodded.

"And don't worry the parents," DI Green said as he gathered up the files on his desk and tucked them under one arm. "Routine enquiry. You know the drill."

As Mackinnon and Collins followed DI Green out of his office, Collins turned to Mackinnon. "Looks like we'll be working overtime tonight, Jack."

CHAPTER TWENTY-NINE

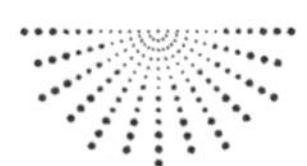

VICTORIA WOKE UP WITH her cheek pressed against the cold stone floor. One of her arms lay trapped beneath her body, and as she stirred, she felt the rush of pins and needles.

She lay on the ground for a moment, blinking up at the light bulb hanging in the centre of the ceiling, and wondered where the hell she was. Then it all came flooding back. The fake audition, the injection… Anya.

She pulled herself up.

"Anya?"

There was no answer.

Victoria got on her hands and knees, ready to crawl towards the corner of the room where Anya was sitting earlier, but something had hold of her leg.

She screamed in terror and tried to scramble away, before realising it was only a rope. She was tied to something. It was hard to see in the dim light. The low wattage light bulb was useless.

She ran her fingers down her leg until they came to rest on the coarse, thin rope and tried to find the knot so she could free herself, but it was hopeless. Maybe she could untie the other end of the rope? She just had to find whatever it was he tied her to. Her fingers ran along the length of the scratchy nylon until they met with a smooth, cold, metal ring bolted to the wall.

He had shackled her to the wall.

A low, terrified moan escaped from her mouth.

"Anya! Anya!" Victoria shouted, panicking. "Where are you?"

"What is it?" Anya asked, her voice sharp with irritation.

"He's tied me to the wall. What should I do?"

Anya was quiet for a moment, then said, "We wait. It's all we can do."

Victoria sat back on her heels. She couldn't just wait. She had to get free and find something she could use as a weapon.

Victoria started to move forward on all fours, spreading her hands to feel over the ground, looking for something… anything she could use as a weapon. She winced as something sharp sliced her palm. She raised it to her mouth and tasted the salty blood. It wasn't a bad cut, but with all the dirt on the floor, it would probably become infected. As soon as she managed to get out of here, she'd get it seen to. It wouldn't be long now.

He'd picked the wrong person to be a victim. Victoria promised herself a long time ago she would never live in fear again. Okay, so her mother had never shown her any affection during her entire miserable childhood, and her stepfather might have knocked her about and used her as a human ashtray. But they did teach her one thing.

Survival.

"Help me, Anya. We need to find something to arm ourselves with so we can fight when he comes back."

Anya didn't answer. She remained hunched over in the corner.

Victoria was starting to lose patience. Couldn't Anya see the danger they were in?

"For God's sake, Anya. What is wrong with you? We need to work together."

"Leave me alone," Anya said. "I don't need to work with you. I don't want to be your friend."

Victoria paused in her search, her hand hovering above the floor. Stung by Anya's words, she blinked back tears, but there was no time for hurt feelings. She took a deep breath.

"Okay, Anya. We don't need to be friends, but we do need to help each other just until we get out of this mess."

"Has he told you what we have to do?" Anya asked, shuffling forward, until Victoria could see her face.

Victoria swallowed and shook her head.

"We are competitors," Anya said. "We put on a show for him."

Victoria waited, from the way Anya spoke, she knew there was more to come.

Anya narrowed her eyes and leaned forward until her forehead was almost touching Victoria's.

"Then he judges us. And do you know what the prize is?" Anya's breath smelt of sour milk and fear.

"No." Victoria's voice came out as a hoarse whisper.

"The winner gets to live," Anya said. "At least, until the next round."

It took Victoria a moment to find her voice. "He won't really do that. He's just trying to scare us."

Anya shook her head. "He means it. This isn't the first time."

"What do you mean?"

Anya leaned back against the padded wall, stared up at the ceiling and muttered something in Polish that might have been a prayer.

She looked back at Victoria and said, "Last time, I won."

CHAPTER THIRTY

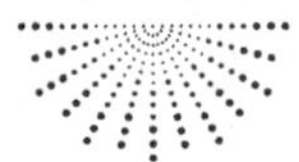

COLLINS PICKED UP THE phone on his desk, his face set in concentration. He spoke quietly, so Mackinnon couldn't hear exactly what he was saying. He tried to gauge Collins' facial expressions, and work out whether it was good news or bad. But Collins kept his face rigid and blank.

He thought about splitting the list with Collins and ringing some of the girls' families himself, but decided visiting Victoria Trent's parents would be more helpful. Her disappearance was recent. Memories and incidents would still be fresh, so there was a much greater chance of getting useful information, some vital clue from them.

The girls on the list had been missing for months. Would the parents remember an odd phone call their daughter received the day she went missing? Or a new friend their daughter might have mentioned? Possibly. But it was more likely that time had dulled the memories, and most of those recollections would be eclipsed by the pain caused by their disappearance.

No, Mackinnon thought, his best chance of getting ahead on this case was dealing with the most recent girls. Anya and Victoria.

Collins, white as a sheet, finished the call. His hand shook as he put down the phone and stared at it for a moment.

"What did they say?" Mackinnon asked.

Collins looked up and gave a half-smile. "That was the first one. Pamela Short. She's all right. She's at home with her little boy. She left the Star Academy after she fell pregnant." Collins held up the list. "You know, Jack. Maybe we are reading too much into this. Maybe they are all fine. I mean, it's like the gym, isn't it? These girls probably signed up for dance classes like people sign up for the gym. Pay for a yearly membership, then never go."

"Maybe," Mackinnon said. "But it doesn't change the fact that Anya Blonski and Victoria Trent are missing."

"No," Collins said, the weak smile slipping from his face.

"I hope you're right though. Maybe these other girls all had genuine reasons for leaving."

Collins didn't answer. He just stared down at the list.

"Will you be all right going through the list on your own?" Mackinnon asked. "I want to go and visit Victoria Trent's parents."

Collins nodded. "Sure. I'll give you a ring as soon as I finish all the calls."

* * *

After Mackinnon left, Collins worked his way steadily through the list of girls. After the first call, his luck ran out. Each conversation, with concerned mothers and fathers asking him for news, crushed him. Every time, Collins heard the tinge of hope in their voices turn to despair when he had to tell them he wasn't calling with good news. But worst of all, was how the hope crept back into their voices at the end of the call. He imagined them thinking no news was good news.

Out of all the girls on the list, only one was safe at home. Probably cuddling her little boy with no idea what had happened to the other girls or what might have happened to her.

He supposed he shouldn't think of them as girls. The youngest on the list was nineteen, and the eldest was twenty-three. They were women. But as Collins got older, he realised just how young nineteen really was.

Collins picked up his mug and took a mouthful of coffee. It was stone cold and made his stomach turn. He felt a lump in his throat and stood up quickly, knocking over his chair.

DC Webb and Lisa, the office manager, looked up, surprised.

"Are you all right, mate?" DC Webb asked.

But Collins didn't answer. He ran out of the room.

Collins didn't stop running until he reached the gents' toilets. Once inside, he locked himself in a cubicle and let the nausea wash over him. He breathed in the air, which was tinged with a strong smell of disinfectant, gulping it down. Slowly, the sick feeling in the pit of his stomach eased.

He unlocked the cubicle door and moved across to the sinks to splash his face with water. He grabbed a bunch of paper towels, dried his face and looked at himself in the mirror.

"Get a bloody grip, you idiot," he muttered.

He hadn't expected his reaction to this case to be so immediate, so visceral.

He regretted not acting on Anya's disappearance sooner, but logically, he knew the way he acted was in line with procedure. He'd done his job. Professionally, he performed the role expected of him. But personally, he felt like he had let Henryk down. If it turned out that these other girls…

Collins shook his head. He wouldn't think about that now. He couldn't. He needed to detach himself. To take this case one step at a time and find Henryk Blonski's sister. He could make it right. He *would* make it right.

With his hair damp and pushed back from his face, Collins returned to the open plan office.

DC Webb walked up to him. "What's up?"

Collins shook his head and placed a hand on his stomach. "Think it's something I ate."

Webb grimaced in sympathy and returned to his own desk.

Collins collected his notes and the list of girls before heading off to find the head of MIT, DCI Brookbank.

He found the DCI in his office, opposite briefing room two. Brookbank was flicking through some sheets of paper when Collins knocked on the open office door.

Brookbank gestured for him to come in. He was a short man, but sturdily built. He reminded Collins of a bulldog.

"I have some paperwork for you, sir," Collins said.

"Regarding the disappearance of Anya Blonski. It seems we might have more missing girls–"

Brookbank held up a hand to cut Collins off. "I am aware of the latest developments. I've spoken to the superintendent. What's this paperwork?"

"A list of names of the girls who are missing and their contact details, along with the notes I made after speaking to their next of kin."

Brookbank nodded. "Thank you. We'll have a briefing in an hour. Can you attend?"

Before he realised what he was doing. Collins shook his head. "I can't, sir. Sorry. I have something I need to do."

Brookbank nodded. "Very well." He lowered his head to resume flicking through the sheets of paper on his desk.

Collins had been dismissed.

Collins left Wood Street Station without telling anyone where he was going. He had a plan. DI Green told him this morning to keep the pressure on Nathan Cleeves, to make him very aware the police were watching him. And Collins intended to do just that. He'd pile on the pressure until Nathan Cleeves squealed.

All the girls had one thing in common: The academy. And Nathan Cleeves was the epitome of a narcissistic bully. It was him. It just had to be.

So if Nathan Cleeves abducted these girls, where was he keeping them? Close to home? He lived above the academy, so it had to be nearby.

Collins felt his hand trembling against the side of his thigh as he walked. He held it up and stared at it. He was literally shaking with anger.

Nathan Cleeves was going to feel pressure, all right. Collins would make sure of that.

CHAPTER THIRTY-ONE

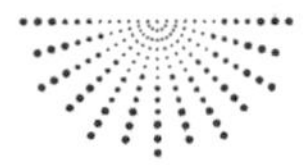

VICTORIA LICKED HER LIPS and tried to swallow as she searched the dark room for a weapon. The rope tied around her leg meant she could only move a metre away from the wall.

"I'm so thirsty," she said.

"So drink," Anya said.

Anya hadn't moved from her position in the corner in ages.

"You said he always drugged the water. I don't want to fall asleep again."

"Isn't it better to sleep than to stay awake through this?" Anya asked, gesturing around the room. "What is there to stay awake for?"

Victoria watched her for a moment. Anya hadn't touched her own water bottle.

Did Anya want her to be drugged? Perhaps so she would have the advantage at competition time...?

No. She couldn't think like that. He couldn't make them compete. She would refuse.

She needed water. Her lips were dry, chapped and painful. She didn't know how long she had been in this room, but thirst burned her throat. Perhaps the thirst was a side effect of the drugs.

She raised the bottle of water to her lips and tried to sip it, fighting the urge to swallow the cool liquid down in one.

Victoria resumed her search, and after five minutes or so, her right hand closed around a solid metal object. She smiled as she weighed it in her hand and ran her thumb along the cylindrical shape. It was some kind of file, made of metal and heavy. She took it back to her side of the room and hid it in the dark shadows by the wall, so it would be within easy reach when she needed it.

She began to feel light-headed and dizzy. The bastard *had* drugged the water again. She reached out her hand for the file. Its cold, hard surface reassured her. Then her head dropped to her chest, and she slept.

On the way to visit Victoria Trent's parents, Mackinnon made use of his Oyster card. There was no point using one of the pool cars, especially at this time of day. He could get there faster using public transport.

He caught the number eight bus from the SY bus stop at St. Paul's. The bus trundled along in the bus lane along Bishopsgate. It took about ten minutes for the bus to slip by the stationary traffic and make it across to Bethnal Green. He got off the bus outside the Bethnal Green Centre, then turned left into Barnet Grove. From there, it was only a five-minute walk to Wellington Row.

Victoria Trent's parents lived in Brabner House, a low-rise block of flats, which sat opposite a row of terraced houses. It was much nicer than the Towers Estate. Each flat had a balcony that faced the road. A few balconies had bikes chained to the railings, and others had washing hanging outside.

The entrance to the flats had a security system. Mackinnon pressed the bell for flat ten. A male voice answered and buzzed him in.

The front door to number ten was open as Mackinnon approached. A skinny man with a shaved head leaned against the doorframe, watching Mackinnon closely.

"Have you got something to tell us about Victoria?" The man chewed his fingernails as he spoke.

"I'm DS Mackinnon." He held out his hand.

The skinny man took it reluctantly and gave it a limp shake. "So what have you got to tell us?"

"Are you Victoria Trent's father?"

"Stepfather." The man corrected Mackinnon. "But I've been on the scene since she was tiny."

"What's your name?"

"Tony. Tony Bryant."

Tony kept his position by the door. It didn't look like Mackinnon was about to be welcomed into the flat with open arms. In fact, it looked as if Tony would prefer him to disappear.

"I'd like to have a chat with you and Victoria's mother. Is it all right if I come in?"

Tony sighed heavily. "Yeah. Go on then. She's out the back. She thought you were bringing bad news."

Mackinnon shook his head. "I don't have any new information to tell you. I spoke to your wife on the phone. We're just trying to track Victoria down. We don't have any reason to believe she's been hurt."

Yet… Mackinnon thought. The words tasted bitter, but he'd assured DI Green he wouldn't say anything to make the missing girls' parents panic.

Tony stood back from the door, allowing Mackinnon to enter the hallway.

"Denise," Tony called, then turned back to Mackinnon. "So what's Victoria done now? What sort of trouble has she got herself mixed up in?"

"It's nothing like that. She's not in any trouble. I just want to ask you a few questions."

"She always was a bloody troublemaker. Never happy unless she was causing some sort of mischief." Tony nodded to the sofa. "Take a seat."

Tony settled back into an armchair, opposite the TV.

After a pointed look from Mackinnon, Tony reached for the remote control and switched it off.

The room was a mess. With their daughter missing, that was understandable. But this mess looked more than a few days old. Dust covered every surface, piles of washing were heaped on chairs and the floor, and there was a lingering smell of mildew, fried food and stale cigarette smoke.

Nothing matched. The sofa was covered in a brown velveteen material, the curtains were orange, and the carpet was a hideous mixture of purple and blue swirls.

It seemed like every home he visited these days had a top-of-the-range, flashy television. It didn't matter about the rest of the house or flat, they might have threadbare carpets, chipped mugs and sagging sofas, but they always had a fancy TV. Victoria Trent's parents had a thirty-two-inch Sony.

"So what do you want to know about Victoria?" Tony asked.

"How long has she been missing?"

"God knows. She's always doing this. She used to run off for days when she got into her teens. Drove her mum round the bend."

"I hoped you and Victoria's mother–"

On cue, Victoria's mother entered the room. She looked like she had a good few years on Tony Bryant. The freshly applied makeup couldn't hide the lines of pain on her face, and the mascara around her eyes only highlighted how red and puffy her eyes were.

"I'm Denise, Vicky's mother," she said, meeting Mackinnon's eyes for only a fraction of a second before turning her gaze to the carpet and its lurid purple and blue pattern.

She moved across to the armchair next to Tony's, picked up the pile of folded washing from the seat and dumped it on the floor. Then she let out a little sob.

"Sorry," she said, dabbing at her eyes with a tissue.

"Don't start the waterworks again, love," Tony said. "That won't help anybody."

Denise sniffed.

Tony slapped the palms of his hands against his thighs. The noise caused his wife to jump.

"He hasn't come with bad news," Tony said, nodding at

Mackinnon, "and it's not as if you'd seen her much over the last couple of years."

Denise stared at Tony with such a burning look of hatred Mackinnon expected him to apologise, but he didn't. Tony carried on, oblivious to his wife's reaction.

"We haven't seen her in years," he said. "So I'm not sure we'll be much use to you."

Denise's lower lip trembled, and she lowered her head to stare at her feet. "She is my daughter, Tony."

"Yeah, I know that," Tony said. The peevish tone of his voice revealed traces of a Birmingham accent. "Not much of a daughter though, is she?"

"Are you telling me that you've had no contact with Victoria, even though you live within walking distance of her flat?" Mackinnon asked. It sounded like an accusation. He didn't mean it that way, but his frustration was rising. It didn't look like Victoria Trent's parents were going to be any use in tracking down the missing girls.

The City of London, the square mile, had a low crime rate, and now, in the space of a couple of days, a man was dead, and girls were disappearing.

Denise didn't speak. She got to her feet slowly as if the weight of the world rested on her shoulders.

Mackinnon watched Denise take a couple of steps over to the fireplace. The fire wasn't alight. They had one of those gas fires that gave the illusion of flames flickering in the background.

One of their neighbours turned a stereo on. The thudding bass seemed loud in contrast to the awkward silence of Victoria Trent's parents' living room.

Denise grabbed a packet of red and white Marlboros

from the mantelpiece. Her hands shook as she tried to pull out a cigarette.

"Something's happened to her," Denise said, looking at Mackinnon.

"We want to find her," Mackinnon said. "Make sure she's okay."

Denise lit a cigarette and held it to her mouth with shaking fingers. She sucked in the smoke hard and held it for a few seconds before exhaling a long plume of smoke.

"I know something's happened. I can feel it."

"Feel it? Don't make me laugh." Tony got out of his armchair and grabbed his jacket. "I'm not sticking around listening to this. You're a hypocrite. You never bloody saw her."

Tony turned to Mackinnon. "You can try and talk to Denise if you want. But I can tell you now, you're wasting your time. We won't be able to help you find her. We've not seen her in years. She hates us."

"She hates you!" Denise screamed to Tony's back as he walked away.

"Not me," she muttered after he'd gone.

After her husband stormed out of the flat, Denise seemed to gather herself together. "I need some air."

She opened the double doors onto the balcony and stepped out. Mackinnon joined her. It was a relief to get out in the fresh air.

"I suppose you think I'm a terrible mother."

"I think you're very upset."

Denise took another puff of her cigarette. "I do see her. Not often, only when Tony's not around. I saw her just a couple of weeks ago, in June."

Mackinnon nodded. "Did she mention anything to you about a new job?"

Denise shook her head and shrugged. "Vicky's head was always full of silly ideas. She wants to be famous. She takes classes, dance classes, I think."

Mackinnon nodded. "At the Star Academy. They told me she missed a class."

Denise scowled. "Not surprised. They're probably worried they won't get anymore money out of her. Do you know how much those classes cost?"

Mackinnon nodded.

"I told her, she'd be better off saving her money, getting a proper job." Denise sighed heavily. "I know I don't sound very supportive, but I just don't want her to be disappointed."

They both stared down at the green area in front of the flats. It was a beautiful day. The sun made even the ugliest areas of the city look decent. A woman walked along the pavement below them, pushing a pram and holding onto a little boy's hand as he toddled along. He was sucking on a purple ice lolly. The sticky juice was smeared around his mouth.

"Maybe it's better to suffer a little disappointment, than never try," Mackinnon said.

The little boy screamed. He'd dropped his lolly on the floor, and his mother wouldn't let him pick it up. She took his hand and pulled him along.

"Is there anyone you can think of who might've held a grudge against her?" Mackinnon asked. "An old boyfriend?"

Denise shook her head. "She's had a few boyfriends

over the years, some serious. But no one recently."

"Why do you think she's gone missing? Do you think she left to work on a cruise ship?"

Denise shook her head and looked down onto the patch of grass below the balcony. "No, I don't. She wouldn't just go off like that and not tell me. I think something bad has happened to her."

She turned to Mackinnon. Tears began to leak from her eyes. "I'm scared I might never see her again."

CHAPTER THIRTY-TWO

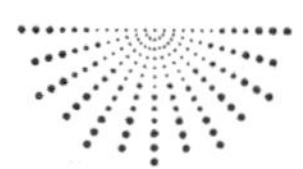

WHEN VICTORIA WOKE UP, she was propped up in a bath, soaking in warm water. Her head lolled back against the taps.

She wasn't alone.

The sick bastard was crouched beside the bath, running a sponge covered with soap suds over her body. Her *naked* body.

Victoria tried to fight him off, but whatever drugs he'd given her were still in her system. Her limbs felt heavy, and she struggled to lift them. Her right arm splashed helplessly back under the water.

"Now, don't get excited, my little star. Save your energy for the competition." He chuckled.

Victoria felt the nausea build and work its way up to her throat. She retched.

"Ugh."

He stood up and grasped Victoria behind the armpits,

lifting her as easily as a doll. The water ran down her body, dripping back into the bath.

"There we are," he said. "All nice and clean."

He bundled her body in a large, white bath towel, threw another smaller towel over her head and began rubbing her hair vigorously.

"You need to look your best tonight, don't you? You're up against last month's champion. I don't mind telling you, I think it's going to be a close one. You both have talent. I can't wait to see which of you triumphs."

He stroked her cheek.

Victoria struggled. She tried to kick him, to raise her hands and gouge his eyes, but her arms were too heavy.

Briefly, she slipped from his grasp, but he caught her quickly, laughing, and said, "You really are something, aren't you?"

Her drug-addled brain was slow to notice her different surroundings, but when she realised she was in a bathroom, her heart leapt. This room wouldn't be soundproofed.

She opened her mouth to scream, but her yell only lasted for a split second. He punched her full in the face.

She couldn't see properly. Dark shapes danced in front of her eyes, and the ringing in her ears went on and on.

She was only vaguely aware of him moving his face close to hers and hissing, "Stupid bitch. Try that again and you're dead."

He scooped her up in his arms, then propped her up on the toilet seat. "I'll put that little outburst down to nerves. First night performances are always the worst, aren't they?"

On the edge of consciousness, she felt him pulling and tugging at her body, smearing stuff on her face.

"We've got to have you looking nice for the camera, haven't we?" he asked, brushing her hair.

He hummed as he worked, applying blusher and lipstick, playing with her like she was the Girls World toy Victoria owned when she was a little girl.

After he finished his role as makeup artist, he stood up and lifted her in his arms. Victoria's head fell backwards. She didn't have the strength to fight. She couldn't even find the energy to keep her eyes open.

She knew he was taking her back to that dark room. She could smell the damp as he carried her closer. She started to cry.

"No tears. You'll ruin your makeup," he said, grinning at her. "Now let's see what Anya thinks of your transformation."

He set Victoria down on the floor, propped up against the wall.

"What do you think, Anya, eh?" he asked as he started to loop the rope around Victoria's ankle. "A stunner, isn't she? I think I've found you a great competitor."

Victoria barely noticed him tightening the rope. Her eyes were fixed on Anya.

Anya was dressed in some kind of ballerina outfit. The clown-like makeup on her face with red circles on her cheeks, terrified Victoria. She looked like a doll possessed by the devil. The dark, black makeup smudged around her eyes only heightened the effect.

Victoria looked down and saw he'd dressed her in a black tutu with yards of netting under the skirt. What the hell was he playing at?

His head bent down as he adjusted Victoria's skirt

around her legs. Victoria reached out her hand and fumbled for the metal file. Her hand closed around it, and she swung it up high, as hard as she could. It felt as if it weighed a ton.

"Screw you," Victoria screamed as she brought the metal file down on him with all her might.

It missed his head, but caught him on the shoulder.

He roared, grabbed the file, ripping it from her hand easily. Then he drew it back and used it to backhand her.

The file connected with her jawbone.

Pain exploded in her jaw. It felt as if her teeth shattered into a million little pieces. Victoria had never felt anything like it.

He grabbed her arms and shook her.

"You ungrateful little bitch! You've been given the opportunity of a lifetime, and you ruined everything.

"I'll have to postpone tonight's performance." He dropped Victoria's arms, and she sprawled on the floor. He pointed at Anya. "You could learn from her. She is a professional. You are an amateur. You'll never amount to anything!"

On the ground, Victoria groaned in pain and rolled her head to the side. From the corner of her eye, in her disorientated state of mind, she thought Anya looked pleased.

CHAPTER THIRTY-THREE

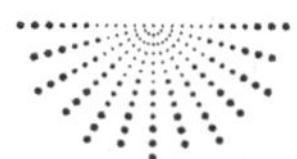

WHEN COLLINS WALKED PAST Oakland's Furniture Store, he saw Fred Oakland in the shop window, rearranging the display. He caught sight of Collins and gave a cheery wave. Collins nodded and walked on to the entrance to the Star Academy.

He told Pippa, the receptionist, he wanted to speak to Nathan Cleeves.

While he was waiting, Collins looked out of the large glass windows. The sun was setting. Above the old buildings and glass skyscrapers, thick streaks of red and gold lined the sky. *Red sky at night, shepherd's delight.* It would be another fine day tomorrow if the glowing sky were any indication.

Could Anya and Victoria see this sunset? Or was it already too late?

He swallowed, and the thought tasted bitter.

"Detective Collins, isn't it?"

Collins turned and saw Roger Cleeves limping down the final steps into the reception area.

"Yes, sir, DC Collins. I actually wanted to speak to your son, Nathan."

Roger Cleeves spread his hands and shrugged. "I'm afraid he isn't here at the moment. He just popped out. He should be back soon, though. Would you like to wait for him upstairs? I could make tea."

Collins nodded. "Thank you."

He followed Roger Cleeves up the three flights of stairs. They made slow progress.

"Where has Nathan gone?" Collins asked.

Roger Cleeves turned on the stairs. "Sorry? What was that?"

"You said Nathan had gone out. I wondered where to."

"Oh, yes, I see. I'm afraid I don't know exactly where he went. He told me he was just going out for a few minutes, so he can't have gone too far."

Roger Cleeves smiled as they finally reached the apartment level. "Here we are," he said and opened the door, allowing Collins to enter the hallway first.

He led Collins to the kitchen. Sitting at the kitchen table, Belinda and Rachel Cleeves were in the middle of a heated discussion.

Collins couldn't work out the subject of their argument before they spotted him and lapsed into an abrupt silence.

"What are you doing here?" Belinda Cleeves asked, her voice full of venom. She rubbed her right foot as she spoke and grimaced.

Her toes were misshapen, twisted and lumpy. That's what years of dancing did for you, Collins supposed. Her feet reminded him of a programme he watched once, which showed how Chinese girls used to have their feet and toes bound, causing them to grow in deformed, narrow stumps, which didn't resemble human feet at all.

Collins looked away. "I'm here to see Nathan," he said.

"I'm afraid he isn't here," Rachel Cleeves said, clutching the neck of her cardigan.

"I'm sure he can see that, Rachel," Belinda Cleeves said, shaking her head at her daughter. "Sometimes you do state the obvious, child."

Rachel Cleeves blushed scarlet and stared down at the table.

Her father put a hand on her shoulder and gave it a gentle squeeze. "The detective is going to have a cuppa while he waits for Nathan to come home."

Roger Cleeves filled the kettle. As he busied himself making the tea, Collins took the opportunity to observe Belinda Cleeves and her daughter. They had an odd relationship. They'd obviously been arguing about something. But what?

Did they know what Nathan had done? Were they involved? It was rare for women to be involved in abductions, but not unheard of.

Clearly irritated by Collins' presence, Belinda Cleeves stood up, grabbed her cup of tea and stalked out of the kitchen.

Rachel looked around nervously for a few moments, before standing up too. "I think I'll go to my room."

"All right, sweetheart. Goodnight," Roger Cleeves said. He handed Collins a mug of tea. "Let's take it into the living room, shall we?"

Collins followed Roger Cleeves into the living room. The room was large, and a three-seater, brown, leather sofa sat opposite the television. A matching two-seater was pushed back against the wall, and two La-Z-Boy reclining armchairs were positioned on either side. Collins sat on one of the armchairs, raised the footrest, settled back and sighed. "Ah, that's better."

The room was dimly lit. An up-lighter lamp in the corner of the room was the only source of light, apart from the bright, coloured lights flickering on the walls and furniture from the television.

A loud, dramatic burst of music prompted Roger Cleeves to pick up the remote control and press the "mute" button.

Collins watched the silent characters on the screen for a few moments, seeing the flashing graphics, and realised it was one of those ubiquitous reality shows.

Roger Cleeves relaxed back into his chair with a contented sigh. "Have you managed to find Anya?"

Collins took a sip of his tea. "We're making progress."

Roger Cleeves nodded. "That's good."

They lapsed into silence for a moment, then Roger Cleeves said. "What was it you wanted to talk to Nathan about?"

Collins chose his words carefully. "I hoped he could help me with a line of enquiry."

"I see. He's not a bad lad, you know. Things were a bit tough for him, after his band, Vivid, split up. It's hard to lose fame and adulation. He got used to it, you see. Believed in the hype."

The minutes ticked past, and Collins glanced at his watch for the second time in the past thirty seconds.

Where the hell was Nathan? Collins was wasting time here. Nathan Cleeves might not be back for hours. If Collins gave up and went back to the station now, he would be in time to attend Brookbank's meeting.

Roger Cleeves' attention had been captured by the reality show again. Light and shapes from the wide, flat-screen TV played across his face.

Collins got to his feet. "I can't wait any longer. When you see your son, Mr. Cleeves, please tell him I want to speak to him."

Roger Cleeves' eyes drifted away from the TV screen. "Of course, I will. I'm sorry. I've no idea what's keeping him."

As Collins shrugged on his suit jacket, he saw Roger Cleeves' eyes widen and his body tense. He'd seen something – someone behind Collins.

Collins spun round. There in the hallway, looking like a kid caught with his hand in the biscuit tin, was Nathan Cleeves.

"Just the man I wanted to speak to," Collins said, staring hard at him.

"What?" Nathan looked at his father, then back to Collins. "I haven't done anything."

"Of course you haven't, son," Roger Cleeves said, easing himself to his feet. He winced as he straightened his knee. "The detective just wants a word, that's all."

Nathan Cleeves backed away, toward the door, bouncing on the balls of his feet.

Collins followed. If Nathan Cleeves wanted to make a run for it, Collins would be ready.

Roger Cleeves obviously saw the panic in his son's eyes and came to the same impression as Collins. "Don't do anything stupid, Nathan. He just wants to chat, that's all."

Nathan spun on his heel, and in an instant, he was out of the apartment door.

Shit.

Collins ran after him.

Behind him, Collins could hear Roger Cleeves calling out, "Don't hurt him. He's just scared. He hasn't done anything wrong."

Collins took the stairs two at a time. Nathan Cleeves was a dancer. He was fit. Face-to-face, fist-to-fist, Collins would win. But running? Stamina wasn't exactly Collins' strongest point. He needed to bring him down quickly.

As he jumped down the final steps and rounded the corner into the reception area, Collins skidded across the polished floor. He scrambled for purchase like a character in a cartoon.

The receptionist looked up from her desk and blinked at him.

"Which way did Nathan Cleeves go?" Collins asked.

The receptionist pointed right, and Collins yanked open the door and stepped out onto the street. His heart was hammering as he looked up the road. It was busy. People were milling about on the pavement, commuters heading home. The sun was low in the sky, dipping behind the buildings, and thick grey clouds had drawn in, threatening rain. So much for the shepherd's weather forecast.

Collins squinted as he searched the crowds. As the

seconds passed, Collins felt the panic begin to build in his chest.

Then he saw him. A flash of yellow.

Collins grinned with relief. Nathan's bright-yellow, zip-up sweatshirt was not the ideal item of clothing to wear if you wanted to blend into a crowd.

Collins' feet pounded hard against the pavement as he chased after Nathan Cleeves. His chest hurt, and already he could feel the start of a stitch, but he wouldn't slow down.

Collins pictured Henryk Blonski lying on the floor of Jubilee House with his head smashed open and dug in harder.

Maybe he'd get into trouble for this. They had no arrest warrant, no interview questions planned, no strategy mapped out, but Collins didn't care about that. He wasn't going to let this bastard disappear, never to face justice. He couldn't bear that.

He screamed at a large woman in a hot-pink skirt-suit to get out of his way. She was dawdling along toward him, tottering on her high heels, searching for something in her bag, oblivious to everyone around her.

Everyone else saw Collins bundling towards them and moved aside. Everyone except that stupid woman.

Collins screamed again, and she looked up, startled, then dropped her phone.

Instead of moving out of his way, she bent down to pick up her mobile, turning sideways so she completely blocked the whole pavement.

Collins was going too fast to slow down. He would have to run into her, or chance the road.

He only had a split second to turn and take a fleeting

glance over his shoulder for traffic before he left the pavement and stumbled onto the road. His ankle twisted as his foot hit the tarmac.

A sharp pain shot up his leg, but Collins ran on.

He couldn't see Nathan Cleeves anymore. He scanned the pavement ahead of him for the yellow sweatshirt.

Where the hell was he? How could he move so quickly?

But he couldn't give up. Collins kept moving, his eyes on the crowds of people around him, trying to catch their faces in case Nathan Cleeves had taken his sweatshirt off. That was just the sort of thing a devious, low-life bastard like him would do.

Then he saw him.

He *had* taken off his sweatshirt, and his arms were pumping at his sides like pistons. Collins felt a jolt of energy. He could do this. He could catch the bastard. There were crowds of people in front, slowing Nathan Cleeves down. He weaved in and out of the commuters. But not quickly enough. Collins was gaining on him.

Collins was so close now. His chest was burning, and his lungs felt like they would burst. He could hear the blood rushing in his ears.

So close. He could almost touch him.

Then Collins saw something Nathan Cleeves hadn't.

A man dressed in a navy, pinstriped suit was striding along the pavement. In one hand, he held his mobile phone up to his ear. In the other, he pulled along a large, black document case on wheels.

Nathan Cleeves had turned, to see how close Collins was, and he hadn't seen the case.

It worked better than Collins dared hope.

Nathan Cleeves tripped over the case, dragging it along with him for a few strides, until finally, he fell forwards onto his hands and knees.

The crowd of commuters gave a collective gasp and stood back, pushing each other in their hurry to get away from the crazy man.

Nathan Cleeves tried to scramble to his feet.

He didn't have a chance. Collins slammed into him. Fourteen stones of pressure flattened Nathan Cleeves to the pavement, winding him.

Collins felt the impact too. The breath left his lungs in a rush. He blinked as dark spots floated before his eyes.

"What the hell? What have you done to my case?" It was the man in the suit.

Collins couldn't talk yet. He didn't have enough air in his lungs.

The man's case lay beneath Nathan Cleeves' body, and Collins could tell it was pretty squashed. He hoped there were only documents in there. He wheezed a couple of times, then gulped down air, but he kept his knee firmly against Nathan Cleeves' back.

"I hope there was nothing breakable in there, sir," Collins said.

"Only paper, but the case cost me a fortune."

"Well, it has..." Collins sucked down another breath of air. "... it has just helped apprehend a suspect."

"Oh, is there a reward for that?"

If it were up to Collins, he would have awarded the case the George Cross. It deserved a bloody medal for bringing Nathan Cleeves down.

Collins ached all over, and his ears were ringing as he

leaned forward, close to Nathan Cleeves' head and said, "Where is she?"

Nathan shook his head and moaned. "Who?"

"You know who I'm talking about. Anya. Where is she?"

Nathan's body shook, and Collins looked down in concern. Maybe he was hurt? Was he having a fit or something?

Collins eased his grip slightly and leaned closer. Then he realised Nathan Cleeves wasn't having a fit.

He was laughing.

CHAPTER THIRTY-FOUR

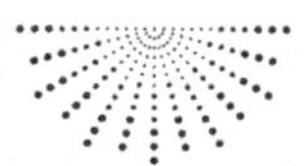

COLLINS STARED IN, WATCHING the interview through the one-way glass. Nathan Cleeves sat at the table, his dark eyes stony and a smirk on his face that turned Collins' stomach.

So far, Nathan Cleeves wasn't talking.

He'd opened his mouth to inform them he didn't want legal representation. Then he shut his mouth and kept it shut for the last thirty minutes.

Collins wiped the sweat from his forehead. Why the hell wasn't he talking? What was he playing at? Collins felt the pressure of the situation start to overwhelm him.

Cleeves ran from him, and Collins reacted by instinct.

By arresting Nathan Cleeves, Collins had shown the police's hand too early. DI Green and DCI Brookbank had been surprised at the speed of Nathan Cleeves' arrest, not to mention unprepared.

To say his superior officers were displeased would be an

understatement. As soon as Collins arrived back at Wood Street Station, DI Green bawled him out. They had nothing on Nathan Cleeves. No evidence. No proof he was connected in any way to the disappearances of Anya Blonski and Victoria Trent.

Collins wanted to search the Cleeves' family flat above the Star Academy and look for the weapon Nathan Cleeves used to kill Henryk Blonski. He thought Nathan Cleeves was the type of killer who would want to keep the weapon as a trophy.

He tried to convince DI Green to apply for a search warrant. But DI Green practically laughed him out of his office, asking him which magistrate would be crazy enough to issue a warrant based on the evidence they had.

Collins should probably have been worrying about his career too. DI Green's furious words wouldn't be the last ear-bashing Collins got this week. He would be on the receiving end of much worse soon enough.

Things would be so much simpler if Nathan Cleeves would start talking. Surely, he couldn't hold out much longer. A man like Nathan Cleeves wouldn't be able to resist the temptation to brag, to let them know how clever he was.

But for now, Nathan Cleeves was keeping his lips tightly closed.

Inside the interview room, Nathan Cleeves raised a bloodied tissue to his face. Collins noticed with satisfaction that Nathan's nose was still bleeding.

DCI Brookbank sat opposite Nathan Cleeves and pushed over a box of tissues. Nathan plucked a fresh one from the box and screwed it up against his nose.

"Would you like to see a doctor about that nose, Nathan?" DCI Brookbank asked.

Nathan narrowed his eyes, then shook his head.

"Speak, you bastard," Collins muttered.

"You better hope, for your sake, he does start to talk," The voice came from behind him.

Collins turned and saw DI Green standing with his hands clasped behind his back.

DI Green didn't look at Collins. He stared straight ahead into the interview room.

"He ran, so I chased him, sir," Collins said, frustrated. "What was I supposed to do? Let him get away?"

DI Green shot him an irritated look but didn't answer.

Inside the interview room, DCI Brookbank was running through the list of charges Nathan Cleeves could face. "… resisting arrest, assaulting a police officer–"

"Assaulting a police officer?" Nathan's face turned purple with rage. "He assaulted me! I should press charges. I was just walking along the street, minding my own business."

"Walking?" Brookbank said. "Come now, Mr. Cleeves, you were running. Trying to evade arrest. We have several witnesses who can confirm that."

Nathan smirked. "Yeah and those witnesses also saw that lunatic jump on top of me. Police brutality, that's what this is. I'm very tempted to take this to the papers. I'm sure they'd be interested."

Brookbank gave Nathan Cleeves a cold smile. "I've a feeling you'll make the papers, Mr. Cleeves, but not like that."

Nathan laughed, then winced and clutched his hand

against his ribs. "You lot think you're so clever, but you haven't got anything on me. You have to charge me in twenty-four hours or let me go." Satisfied, Nathan Cleeves nodded to himself and leaned back in his chair.

His smug expression made Collins want to slam his fist into Nathan Cleeves' face.

Beside Collins, DI Green muttered, "Someone's been watching a lot of cop shows on television."

DCI Brookbank got to his feet slowly. He stared down at Nathan Cleeves. "I'll be back."

For the first time, Collins felt a glimmer of hope. It wasn't so much what Brookbank said, but the way he said it. Confident and in control. Brookbank was good at this.

Nathan Cleeves smiled. "I'll be waiting," he said and winked at Brookbank.

But his bravado was betrayed by a tremor in his voice. Nathan Cleeves' confidence was slipping away. Collins could tell he was worried by the way his eyes followed Brookbank to the door.

Yes, Brookbank was good. Collins just hoped, for Anya and Victoria's sake, he was good enough.

CHAPTER THIRTY-FIVE

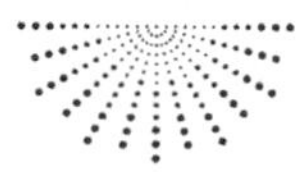

WHILE BROOKBANK LEFT NATHAN to sweat in the interview room, Collins decided to call Mackinnon. He couldn't put it off any longer.

"I've messed up, Jack," Collins said as soon as Mackinnon answered his call.

"What? Why? What's happened?"

"He ran," Collins said. "Why would he run if he didn't have anything to hide? Tell me that."

"Who ran? You're not making any sense, Nick."

"Nathan Cleeves. I brought him in for questioning."

"Is he talking?"

"Not yet. And Brookbank's on the war path. He wants my blood. I think I've pretty much blown my chance of getting into MIT with this."

"Hang on. Let's not get this out of proportion. He ran," Mackinnon said. "If you'd let him get away you'd probably be in trouble for that too."

Collins exhaled heavily and tugged at the spiral telephone cord attached to the handset. "DI Green said the same thing. He's pretty pissed off with me, but he is doing his best to back me up. But up against Brookbank, I don't like my chances."

Collins waited, but Mackinnon didn't reply. He heard the buzz of traffic on the phone line.

"MIT are trying to question him now," Collins said. "I know it's him, but he won't talk."

"Give MIT time," Mackinnon said. "They know what they're doing."

Collins heard a loud rumble of thunder over the phone line. "Where are you? Did you speak to Victoria Trent's parents?"

"Yeah. I just left. If there were an award going for awful parents of the year, I think they'd be in the running. I can't work them out. Her mother seems cut up, but it is almost as if her stepfather doesn't care. He's just not bothered. I don't know whether that is because he believes she is safe and just gone off on her own… Apparently, it isn't unheard of for her to do that, but still, I expected a little concern."

* * *

After Mackinnon finished the call with Collins, he hunched his shoulders and looked up at the sky. Dark storm clouds were gathering fast, closing in on the City. Just a few minutes ago, the sky had been clear. He heard a deep rumble of thunder as the first few drops of soft rain hit his face.

The situation had changed rapidly now that Nathan Cleeves was in custody. If they were going to make a charge stick, a charge the CPS wouldn't laugh out of court, they needed evidence.

Victoria Trent's family were a dead end. He couldn't get any leads from them. Anya's parents were flying over from Poland, so it would be a few hours before he could talk to them. Although he knew he couldn't count on them to provide many clues.

Mackinnon rubbed his forehead and took a deep breath, trying to ward off the headache he felt building behind his eyes. The air was thick with the prickly scent of ozone.

Mackinnon quickened his pace. He would pay another visit to Rachel Cleeves at the Star Academy before heading back to the station. If her brother had taken these girls, surely she would have noticed something. She seemed like a decent person, and more importantly, she seemed to trust him.

Mackinnon started to run as the rain shot down like needles. He sprinted past Oakland's Furniture Shop, where Fred Oakland was rearranging the window display.

By the time he reached the Star Academy, and pressed the bell, Mackinnon was drenched. His soaked cotton shirt clung to his skin, and rainwater trickled down from his hair into his eyes.

The receptionist's eyes widened as he entered. "Oh, is it raining?"

"Just a bit," Mackinnon said, running his hand back and forth through his hair, to try and get rid of some of the water. "Is Rachel around? I'd like a quick word if she is."

The receptionist smiled and picked up the phone. Before she had a chance to dial, there was a clattering sound on the stairs.

Belinda Cleeves appeared. "I thought it was you. I saw you on the security cameras. You have a nerve coming here."

"I hoped I could talk to your daughter," Mackinnon said.

"No, you cannot." Belinda Cleeves strode across the foyer. "I don't believe it. You've arrested my son, and then you have the audacity to come and visit my daughter."

Mackinnon frowned. He thought Belinda Cleeves had the wrong end of the stick. "It's not a social call. It relates to our enquiry into Anya Blonski's disappearance."

The receptionist squeezed past them. "I'll be off now then. Goodnight."

She opened her umbrella by the front door, then after waiting for a response from Belinda Cleeves and not getting one, she gave a little shrug and walked out, closing the door behind her.

"I don't care. You can't see Rachel. I forbid it." Belinda Cleeves craned her neck to look up at Mackinnon. "And I hope you realise you've made a terrible mistake. My son would never hurt anyone."

Mackinnon thought back to the circular bruises he'd seen on Nathan's girlfriend's arms. "In that case, he doesn't have anything to worry about."

A clap of thunder made Belinda Cleeves tense. Heavy rain hammered down on the window.

Two small scarlet patches appeared in the middle of

Belinda Cleeves' pale cheeks. "The little bitches. Those girls ran off to work on a cruise ship. Why have you arrested my son for that?"

"There are seven girls missing, Mrs. Cleeves. Doesn't that strike you as odd? All of them from your Star Academy."

A creaking noise made them both turn. A door underneath the stairs slowly opened.

Roger Cleeves appeared in the doorway.

Mackinnon stared at him. There was something strange, something different about Roger Cleeves. But Mackinnon couldn't put his finger on it. What was it?

Conflict flickered across Roger Cleeves' face. He quickly adjusted his expression, but not quickly enough.

"What's down there?" Mackinnon asked, looking past Roger Cleeves and through the doorway.

"Down there? Nothing. Only the furniture store basement. Storage."

"Why were you down there?"

Alarm bells were screaming in Mackinnon's mind. He could hear the blood rushing in his ears.

"I was just chatting to Fred, the furniture guy," Roger Cleeves said. "There's no law against that, is there?"

Mackinnon forced a smile, even managed to choke out a laugh. "Not as far as I am aware."

Roger Cleeves smiled and put his arm around his wife. "Come on, love. I know you're worried, but there's no need. Nathan will be back home before you know it."

He kissed his wife's cheek, then looked at Mackinnon. "I take it you can find your own way out?"

Mackinnon nodded and headed towards the door.

Roger Cleeves was lying.

Just before he entered the academy, Mackinnon had seen Fred Oakland in the window of his shop, and Roger Cleeves had not been with him.

CHAPTER THIRTY-SIX

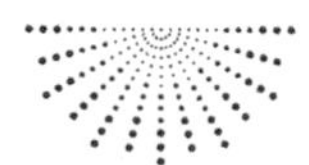

MACKINNON WENT STRAIGHT TO Oakland's and tapped on the glass door. The rain was still hammering down, and Mackinnon kept as close to the shop window as possible, trying to stay dry under the small awning. The sign hanging from the door was flipped over to the "Closed" side, and most of the lights inside were switched off.

Mackinnon knocked again. Fred Oakland was here only a few moments ago, surely he hadn't just missed him.

There was a movement inside the shop. Mackinnon was in luck.

Fred Oakland walked up to the door with a pile of paperwork in his hands and a frown on his face. When he saw Mackinnon waiting outside, he unbolted the door and opened it.

"I was just about to go home," Fred Oakland said.

"Can I come in?" Mackinnon asked. "Just for a minute?"

Fred Oakland sighed and opened the door wider. "All right. What can I do for you? Is this still about the missing girl?"

Fred Oakland walked back to the counter and dumped the stack of paperwork by the till. "I can't help you on that score, I'm afraid. I did see your colleague this afternoon. What was his name?"

"DC Nick Collins?"

"Ah, yes that was it. I hoped he was coming back as a customer, but unfortunately not. I don't suppose you're here to buy something else?"

Mackinnon shook his head.

"Pity." Fred Oakland pointed to the window display. "I'm trying something new, trying to attract some passing trade." He shrugged. "Well, you have to try, don't you?"

"I need to ask you about the areas of this building you rent out to the Star Academy."

Fred Oakland blinked a couple of times. "Oh, I see. Okay. Well, they have the top four floors. Three for the academy and the top floor for their living quarters."

"And downstairs? A building like this must have a basement."

Fred Oakland nodded slowly. "Yes. I store some of my furniture down there. They've rented a small area of the basement, but they never seem to use it."

"Do you know why they needed storage in the basement?" Mackinnon asked.

Fred Oakland shook his head. "No. Roger Cleeves mentioned something about a recording studio. I don't really pay much attention. To tell the truth, I'm regretting letting it out to them now. It sounds like a bloody herd of elephants upstairs when they have their dance classes. It puts my customers off. Well, it would if I had any."

Fred Oakland punched a couple of buttons on the till and the drawer opened. He started to cash up, counting notes.

"So Roger Cleeves uses the downstairs as a recording studio? Does his son, Nathan use it?"

"Yeah. I'm sure that's what he said it would be used for. He converted one of the larger of the storage rooms into a recording studio, or some such nonsense. I didn't want to rent out any of the basement at first, but he offered me good money."

Fred Oakland stopped counting the ten-pound notes and rubbed the side of his nose. "He must have spent a fair bit of money on it too. He had it soundproofed and everything, but I've never seen anyone using it. Waste of money, if you ask me. Still, I'm glad he got it soundproofed. I wouldn't have any customers left if I had that lot wailing down there every day."

Mackinnon grabbed his phone and dialled Collins' number. While the phone rang, he asked Mr. Oakland, "Do you have a key?"

Oakland frowned. "For the recording studio?"

Mackinnon nodded.

"Um, yes, I have one somewhere. Do you want it now?"

"Yes."

Collins finally answered as Mr. Oakland rummaged around in the cupboard beneath the till.

CHAPTER THIRTY-SEVEN

MACKINNON WALKED TOWARD THE door, away from Fred Oakland, and keeping his voice low, he brought Collins up to speed.

"He's looking for the key to the basement room now," Mackinnon said. "It might be nothing, but I thought I'd better let you know."

"Do you need backup?" Collins asked.

Mackinnon paused for a beat, then said, "No. I'll call you if I find anything. How are things going with Nathan Cleeves?"

Collins sighed loudly. "He's still not talking. DCI Brookbank's planning the strategy for a third interview now. But it's not looking good."

Fred Oakland chuckled, and Mackinnon turned and saw him waggling the key.

"Look, I've got to go now, Nick," Mackinnon said. "But I'll keep you posted."

"All right, I'll leave now. I'm not much use hanging around the station. I can be with you in ten minutes."

Fred Oakland beamed at Mackinnon as he clutched the key in his podgy fist. "Found it," he said. "I knew I had it somewhere."

"Great," Mackinnon said. "Let's go and take a look."

The smile slid from Fred Oakland's face. "You want to open it now?"

"Yes."

Fred Oakland frowned. "Shouldn't we check with Mr. Cleeves first?"

"Absolutely not."

Mr. Oakland shrugged and led the way through the shop to an old door set into the back wall. The frame was small, and Mackinnon had to duck as he walked through the doorway.

The musky smell of fresh wood shavings wafted along the corridor.

"This is the entrance to the basement," Fred Oakland said. "There's another entrance, in the Star Academy's reception."

Mackinnon nodded. He'd seen it and watched Roger Cleeves stroll out of the basement less than ten minutes ago.

Fred Oakland opened the door to the basement. Mackinnon could see the first couple of steps leading downwards, but the rest of the stairs were hidden by the darkness.

Fred Oakland ran his hand along the wall just at the entrance, trying to locate a light switch. When he found it, he turned the light on with a snap.

A single light bulb hung down over the staircase. The

light wasn't powerful, perhaps a forty-watt bulb, and the edges of the steps remained in shadow.

The gentle hum of electricity made Mackinnon wonder how many years it had been since the electrics in this place were updated.

Fred Oakland turned to Mackinnon and smiled. "I'll go first, shall I?"

Mackinnon nodded but couldn't smile back. His mouth was dry, and the damp smell drifting up from the basement made his skin crawl. Fred Oakland led the way down the stone steps.

"You'll need to watch your footing," Fred Oakland said. "The damp can make the stairs slippery."

Mackinnon reached out for the wall, pressed his hand against the rough stone work and steadied himself. After a few more steps, Mackinnon felt something touch the skin on the back of his hand. He yanked back his arm, but it was only a cobweb. He wiped it away and continued down the steps.

When they reached the bottom of the stairs, Fred Oakland disappeared around a corner. Mackinnon followed quickly, not wanting to be left behind down here. The smell of damp grew stronger as they walked along a narrow corridor. The only source of light was the solitary light bulb over the staircase, and as they walked away from it, Mackinnon found it more and more difficult to keep up with Fred Oakland.

Mackinnon caught his foot and stumbled. He held out his hands to break his fall, grazing his palms. He wiped them on his trousers and shivered as he heard a scratching sound and imagined rats scurrying past. When he looked up again, he couldn't see Fred Oakland.

Shit. Mackinnon pulled out his mobile phone, and used the light from it to get a better look at his surroundings. The walls were a light brown, spotted with darker patches, perhaps from water damage or damp. Further along the corridor, the damp was worse. It streaked the walls, leaving marks behind like dripping, black treacle. Mackinnon looked down and saw what tripped him up: a large stone brick. Mackinnon nudged it with his foot so it sat back against the wall, out of the way.

"Detective?" Fred Oakland's voice drifted along the corridor.

"Coming." Mackinnon walked forward, using the light from his mobile phone to guide him.

As he walked around the next corner, he saw Fred Oakland hunched over next to a black door. He waited as Fred Oakland jiggled the key in the lock.

Then Fred Oakland turned around, and Mackinnon almost jumped out of his skin.

The pupils of Fred Oakland's eyes were huge. They looked like dark stones set in his pale round face. It made Mackinnon's skin crawl.

He knew it was just due to the lack of light down here. Mackinnon's own pupils would look the same, but he felt an overwhelming desire to get out of this basement and away from Fred Oakland.

Fred Oakland held the key up close to his face and peered at it, frowning.

"That's funny," he said.

"What is?"

"The key doesn't fit."

"Try it again."

Mackinnon's heart was thumping; he just knew there was something behind this door. Something Roger Cleeves was hiding from them. Was he protecting his son?

Fred Oakland leaned forward again to put the key in the lock. He tried turning clockwise, then anticlockwise, but it didn't move.

"It's no good." Fred Oakland straightened. "He must have had the locks changed."

Mackinnon hit the door with his fist.

"Temper, temper..." The voice came from behind them, making both Mackinnon and Fred Oakland turn around.

Roger Cleeves stood on the bottom step, his face half covered by shadow.

"Hey, Cleeves! What's the big idea?" Fred Oakland asked. "I never gave you permission to change the locks."

"Oh, didn't you?" Roger Cleeves stared at Oakland, a small smile playing on his lips.

"No. You know I bloody well didn't." Fred Oakland pointed at Cleeves with the key. "Now open up this door."

"Why?"

Fred Oakland put his hands on his hips and shook his head so hard his cheeks wobbled. "Why? I'll tell you why. Because this gentleman is a police officer, and he wants to take a look inside."

Fred Oakland moved forward, standing chest to chest with Roger Cleeves, scowling in his face.

"Stand back, please, Mr. Oakland," Mackinnon said.

But Fred Oakland ignored him. He poked Roger Cleeves in the chest with his finger, "Open up."

"Take a step back, please, Mr. Oakland," Mackinnon said.

But it was too late.

In a flash, Roger Cleeves had a switch blade held against Fred Oakland's fleshy throat.

"I think I'll be going now, Detective," Roger Cleeves said, backing out of the passage, moving towards the stairs leading up to the furniture store.

Taking his time, he walked backwards, holding Fred Oakland close to him and keeping his knife tight against the man's neck.

All at once, it became clear.

The fragments came together, and Mackinnon realised what had seemed off earlier when he entered the Star Academy reception from the basement. This was not a man crippled by arthritis. He stood erect, walking easily and fluidly. He didn't have a limp. It was all an act, a show put on for their benefit. Mackinnon's mind spun in a million directions, all at once.

Mackinnon's mobile rang, piercing the tension.

Roger Cleeves slowly shook his head. "Don't even think about it. Let it ring. If you call for help, or follow me, I'll slit his throat."

Mackinnon stared after them, watching them move closer to the exit. He wasn't afraid anymore. He was furious.

Adrenaline was coursing through his veins, filling him with rage.

He stayed frozen to the spot until they disappeared. He could hear Fred Oakland whimpering. Mackinnon's fingers closed around his mobile phone. He'd wait a few more seconds, until Roger Cleeves was out of earshot, then he'd call it in.

There was no way in hell Roger Cleeves was going to get away with this.

Mackinnon stared at the door Fred Oakland had been trying to unlock. It was huge and nothing like the other doors in the building. The door from the furniture store to the basement was old and flimsy. This door was strong and looked new and sturdy.

What was Roger Cleeves hiding?

Were Anya and Victoria locked in there, still alive?

Mackinnon slammed into the door with his shoulder, grunting with the effort. Pain shot along his arm, but the door didn't budge. He kicked out, aiming for the lock. The thud echoed around the basement but still, the door didn't move.

Mackinnon was a big guy, but there was no way he was going to be able to move that on his own. They'd need a team with tools to get it open.

Mackinnon crouched on the floor, heart pounding, trying to catch his breath. How long had it been? Long enough, he decided and grabbed his phone, dialling Collins.

No answer.

Shit. Why wasn't he answering?

He dialled DI Green's number.

When the detective inspector answered, Mackinnon said, "It's the old guy. Nathan's father, Roger Cleeves. He has a knife and he's taken Fred Oakland hostage."

"Slow down, Jack," DI Green said. "Tell me everything."

CHAPTER THIRTY-EIGHT

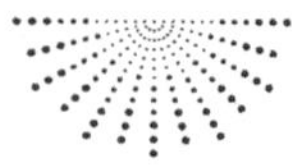

AFTER HE'D EXPLAINED THE situation to DI Green, Mackinnon raced upstairs. He paused by the door to the furniture store.

Had Roger Cleeves already left?

No. Mackinnon could hear voices.

He pushed himself back against the wall, slid slowly up to the door frame and peered into the shop floor. The fluorescent lights shone brightly, illuminating the furniture. In the middle of the store, Roger Cleeves stood with one arm gripping Fred Oakland's torso tightly.

Mackinnon couldn't see his other hand, but he was pretty sure Roger Cleeves still had the knife.

Mackinnon shifted his gaze, looking for something he could use as a weapon. His eyes fixed on a small wooden stool. Maybe he could use that to defend himself if Cleeves lunged at him with the knife.

Then Mackinnon heard a familiar voice.

His head shot up.

Collins stood in the shop doorway, his hands raised in a placatory gesture.

"Don't come any closer," Roger Cleeves said.

No one seemed to notice Mackinnon. He slowly started inching his way towards them. If he could just get to the counter...

"P... please..." Fred Oakland clasped his hands together in front of his face as if he were praying, begging.

Mackinnon moved to just behind the service counter and peered out from behind the till. He could only see their legs from his position.

"Please don't hurt me..." Fred Oakland moaned. A yellow puddle spread at his feet.

"Oh, Christ. That is disgusting." Roger Cleeves stepped back just a fraction, to avoid the pool of urine.

He loosened his grip on Fred Oakland, moving the knife away from his throat.

This was Mackinnon's chance.

He moved forward.

But Roger Cleeves heard him. He swung around to face Mackinnon.

"Well, well, it seems you didn't listen to me. Did you think I wouldn't keep my word?"

Cleeves dug the knife into Fred Oakland's throat. Beads of blood appeared along the surface of the cut.

Jesus, for one horrifying moment, Mackinnon thought he was going to slit the man's throat in front of them.

In the next fraction of a second, he caught Collins' eye and some kind of understanding passed between them.

Collins and Mackinnon both ran at Roger Cleeves, Collins yelling at the top of his lungs.

They connected. A flash of colour.

During training, they were lectured on the acceptable level of violence an officer could use to overpower a suspect. Each individual case might warrant a different level of force, but it should always be *controlled* force.

In theory, Mackinnon agreed. He had little time for officers who abused their power, and there was a fine line between subduing a suspect and what some might call police brutality. But face-to-face with a man trying to stab him, Mackinnon's instinct took over.

He felt Roger Cleeves' soft flesh yield beneath his fists as he punched, again and again. He waited, expecting to feel the sharp blade of the knife at any moment. His body tensed for the blow.

Where was it? Where the hell was the knife?

Collins had his hands around Roger Cleeves' throat. His face was turning purple. Collins was still hollering, screaming a string of intelligible swear words.

The knife, Mackinnon had to get the knife.

He saw the flash of the blade as Roger Cleeves swiped it inches from Collins' face. Mackinnon made a grab for it.

His hand closed around Roger Cleeves forearm, and Mackinnon pulled back so hard, Cleeves squealed like a stuck pig.

The knife clattered to the floor, and Mackinnon kicked it away.

"Stay down," Collins growled as Roger Cleeves squirmed on the floor.

Mackinnon kept his knee on the man's back until Collins cuffed him.

"My arm, you bastard," Roger Cleeves screamed. "You've broken my sodding arm."

Mackinnon ignored him.

He turned to Fred Oakland, who was curled up in the corner of the room, his eyes wide and staring, watching Collins make the arrest.

Mackinnon moved across, knelt beside him, put a hand on his shoulder. "Are you all right, mate?"

Fred Oakland nodded.

Mackinnon's legs felt too weak to support him as he tried to stand. "No injuries?"

"Yeah," Roger Cleeves yelled. "My arm!"

"I wasn't talking to you."

Fred Oakland shook his head. "I'm fine."

Mackinnon stared down at Roger Cleeves. His shoulder was at a funny angle, most likely dislocated rather than broken. There was probably something in the rule book that said they were supposed to un-cuff him, but sod that. The cuffs were staying on.

"I need the key for that room." Mackinnon said. "Search his pockets."

"Here. Try these," Collins said, throwing a key ring full of keys at Mackinnon.

Mackinnon turned his head towards the window as he heard sirens approaching.

"We should wait." Collins said.

But Mackinnon was already heading for the basement.

CHAPTER THIRTY-NINE

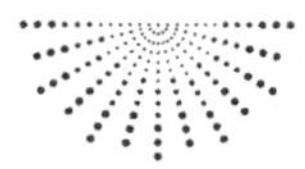

HEADING BACK DOWN INTO the dark, dank basement, Mackinnon felt an undeniable sense of dread. There was something evil about this place, something that made him want to run out of here and not look back.

He took a deep breath and continued on down the dimly lit, narrow corridor, following the twists and turns, using the light of his mobile phone to guide him like before until he reached the huge black door. He hammered on it with the side of his fist.

"Hello? Is anyone in there? Can you hear me?"

He listened for a reply while fumbling for the keys, but heard nothing.

There were six keys on the key ring. He went for the biggest one first, stabbing it towards the lock, but it was too big. The second one he chose fitted into the keyhole but wouldn't turn.

The third fitted perfectly, and as he turned the key, he heard the clunk of the lock mechanism moving.

He pushed the door hard. It was heavy, and obviously reinforced. As the door creaked open, the smell of sweat, unwashed bodies, fear and something else… flooded over him. Bile rose in his throat, and sweat drenched his body.

"It's the police," Mackinnon said as he edged inside the room. "Is anyone in here?"

The room was in complete darkness, and he shone the light from his mobile phone into the room as he fumbled along the wall, looking for a light switch.

The light from the mobile phone flickered over large pieces of equipment: cameras, amplifiers and what looked like a stage. It was an eerie sight.

There was no response. Was the room really only used for storage? Then where was that terrible smell coming from? And why did Roger Cleeves panic when Mackinnon wanted to look inside?

Something lying on the ground caught Mackinnon's left foot, causing him to stumble. He swore. What was that? It felt soft. He leaned closer but could only make out a dark shape. As he shone the light from his mobile on the ground to see what it was, the light shone over a body, and two eyes stared up at him.

He felt as if he'd been punched in the gut. He doubled over, the air left his lungs, and he gasped for breath.

Then the body on the ground screamed.

Jesus. She was still alive.

"It's all right," Mackinnon said. "I'm a police officer. You're safe now."

He moved towards the figure on the floor and held her hand. The screaming subsided and turned into gentle sobs.

"What's your name, sweetheart?"

After a pause, a voice from behind answered. "I am Victoria Trent. That is Anya Blonski. He wouldn't let us go."

Mackinnon turned, but he couldn't see the speaker in the darkness. "It's okay, Victoria. We're going to get you out of here."

He shone the light from his phone along Anya's body. He couldn't see very well, but he could see the blue, nylon rope binding her wrists together.

Mackinnon plucked at the knot. His fingers felt too big and clumsy, but he finally managed to untie the ropes.

He stayed crouched next to Anya, holding her hand until he heard footsteps behind him.

Someone switched on a portable floodlight. Mackinnon blinked at the sudden dazzling brightness.

Someone swore.

Mackinnon looked down at Anya lying in front of him. Her face was bruised and swollen. He turned and saw Victoria huddled against the base of one of the cameras. Jesus. She was tied to the wall.

Mackinnon couldn't take it all in. They were both wearing some kind of freaky stage costumes. He'd dressed the girls up like ballerinas. Their faces were painted with a Barbara Cartland amount of makeup, but it couldn't hide the bruises. And the makeup on Anya's face had run where tears had streaked down her face.

DI Green's hand patted his back. "All right, Jack."

Two female paramedics entered the room, and spoke in soothing voices. It was only then that it occurred to Mackinnon maybe he should have waited. A man barrelling into the room in the dark probably scared them even more. He should have listened to Collins.

Collins? Mackinnon looked around and saw Collins standing in the doorway, his face deathly pale. He slapped a hand over his mouth and backed away.

One of the female paramedics crouched down next to Anya. She smiled gently at Mackinnon and reached across to take Anya's small hand from his. Anya gripped his hand tightly, and Mackinnon was surprised to feel he didn't want to let go.

"You'll be okay now, Anya. You're safe," he said and pulled his hand away.

"I'll take care of her now," the female paramedic said as she began to treat Anya, talking to her all the time, explaining exactly what was happening and what she was going to do next.

Mackinnon stood up and felt strangely detached as he looked around the room, which was slowly filling up.

Blue-suited CSIs waited outside, anxious to get started. DI Green was in conversation with the paramedic treating Victoria. The feeling of dread hadn't abated. It was steadily building, crushing the air from his lungs.

Mackinnon backed out of the room.

He found Collins on the street outside the academy.

"Are you okay, Nick?"

Collins blinked and swallowed hard. "Yeah, it's just. They're alive, you know? And I thought, I thought…"

Collins repeatedly kicked the stone steps in front of the academy, scuffing his black leather shoes. Mackinnon watched him struggling to keep his composure.

"I know, Nick."

"We saved them, though. They're okay," Collins said. He puffed out his cheeks and exhaled heavily. "Sorry." He waved a hand. "Ignore me. I'm going soft in my old age."

Collins seemed short of breath as he struggled to find the right words. "I didn't realise. I think I was blaming myself, you know. For not acting sooner, for not listening to that poor bastard, Henryk. But they're alive. I mean, thank God. I don't know what I would have done if… if…" Collins broke off and stared at Mackinnon. "Why are you looking at me like that?"

Mackinnon waited a beat. He didn't know how to say what he needed to.

"What is it, Jack? What's the matter?"

"Didn't you smell it?"

Collins shook his head. "No you're wrong," he said, his voice ragged and raw. "The smell was because the girls were in there for days with no toilet, nowhere to wash…"

Mackinnon stayed silent, but Collins doubled over as if Mackinnon had hit him.

"No. You're wrong. They're all right." He clutched Mackinnon's arm. "You're wrong."

Mackinnon said nothing, just looked down at Collins.

Collins stared up at him with bloodshot eyes. "Oh, Jesus, Jack."

CHAPTER FORTY

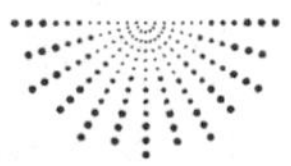

FEELING USELESS, MACKINNON PATTED Collins on the back. "All right, Nick. Take it easy. Stay out here."

He angled Collins and pushed him down to sit on the stone steps.

Collins pulled his knees up to his chest and rested his head on his arms. Mackinnon sat beside him. They sat there for a while, staring at the streetlights reflected in the puddles on the pavement, not speaking because there wasn't much to be said. Nothing that would help anyway.

After five minutes or so, Mackinnon heard a clattering behind them. They stood up and moved to the side as the paramedics wheeled Anya out on a stretcher.

Her eyes were wide and blinking as they met Mackinnon's.

"I … Wait. I need to talk to him." Anya struggled to sit up on the stretcher.

"Careful, my love," one of the paramedics said, reaching

out to steady her. "You can speak to him later after you've been checked out at the hospital."

"No," Anya insisted. "Now. Victoria told me Henryk was looking for me. Henryk, my brother? Can you tell him I'm safe?"

Mackinnon couldn't speak. Words formed in his head, but he couldn't force them past the lump in his throat. She didn't know her brother was dead, probably murdered by Roger Cleeves.

Mackinnon was saved by a woman running along the pavement, calling Anya's name.

Anya turned. "Mama?" Tears rolled down her cheeks as her mother embraced her.

The paramedics looked on bemused, as a middle-aged man, Mackinnon guessed to be Anya's father, joined the hug.

Collins stared at the family group. "He looks like Henryk," he said.

Another lady walked up to the group and smiled. She leaned close to Mackinnon and held out her hand. "I'm Milena Pawlak, the interpreter."

Mackinnon introduced himself and Collins.

Then Milena spoke a few words in Polish to the Blonskis. Mackinnon only recognised one: *Policja*. Police.

Mrs. Blonski turned to Mackinnon and Collins. She reached for their hands and looked up at them with tears in her eyes.

"I'm so sorry," Collins stammered.

"I'm afraid Anya's parents can't speak English," the interpreter said.

But Mrs. Blonski didn't need words to express how she

felt. The pain reflected in her eyes. She smiled at them, but her smile was stiff and full of anguish.

She said, *"Dziekuje po tysiackroc."*

Milena turned to Mackinnon and Collins, smiling. "Mrs. Blonski said, 'Thank you. A thousand times, thank you'."

* * *

Mackinnon watched them load Anya and Victoria into separate ambulances, then he said to Collins, "I'm going back inside. Will you be all right?"

Collins nodded, his eyes fixed on a couple of office workers, leaving the Golden Fleece pub, opposite, and walking back towards the tube.

When Mackinnon returned to the basement, he could see DI Green had it all under control, his steely eyes sweeping the room as he barked out orders.

The room looked very different now that bright crime scene lights illuminated every nook and cranny of the garish chamber. Mackinnon's stomach churned as his eyes focused on the shackles on the wall.

He took a deep breath and felt his mouth fill with a smell so strong he could taste it.

It still lingered in the air: the heavy, cloying odour of death.

Mackinnon walked across to DI Green. "Anything out of Cleeves, sir?"

DI Green nodded. "He's not talking. Waiting for his legal rep."

Mackinnon swore.

"Don't worry, Jack. He won't get away with this." DI

Green ran a hand through his white hair. "Mr. and Mrs. Blonski flew in from Poland tonight. I've organised a car to take them to the hospital to see Anya."

Mackinnon nodded. "I saw them outside."

"Over here, sir," one of the scene of crime officers called out to DI Green.

Mackinnon realised he was holding his breath. He didn't want to follow DI Green, but he fell into step beside him, pulled by some unseen force.

One of the other officers gagged, and the bile rose in Mackinnon's throat.

"How many?" DI Green asked, his voice cold and detached.

The SOCOs had pulled away the soundproofing in one corner of the room and opened up a cavity in the wall. One of the officers stood on tiptoe, pointing his torch into the hole and peering inside.

"Can't say yet," he said. "Could be five or six. We'll have to get the bodies out of here. It looks like he stacked them one on top of the other."

Mackinnon sensed a movement in the doorway. He turned to see Collins looking into the room in horror.

Collins caught Mackinnon's eye then slowly turned and walked away.

* * *

Half an hour later, Mackinnon found Collins outside, leaning back against the red-brick wall. He had a cigarette in his hand.

"I didn't know you smoked," Mackinnon said.

"I don't. At least, I haven't for eight years."

Mackinnon leaned back on the wall beside him.

"We were too late," Collins said. "I should have listened to Henryk when he first came in. I should…"

"Those girls down there have been dead a long while, Nick. It wouldn't have made a difference."

Collins stared down at the floor. "I'm not so sure about joining MIT now. I think I'd prefer to give this up altogether."

They stared out at the road as two men walked out of the Golden Fleece pub and flagged down a black cab.

"Maybe I'll get a job as a taxi driver," Collins said and gave a weak grin.

Mackinnon smiled back. "You'd be rubbish at that. You drive like an old lady."

Collins gave him a playful punch on the arm, then they stood in silence for a moment.

"We stopped him," Collins said. "He won't be able to do it anymore. That's good, right?"

"Yeah." Mackinnon nodded. "That's good."

CHAPTER FORTY-ONE

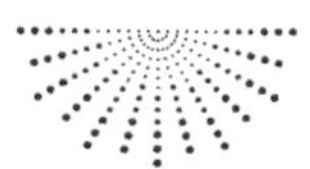

A WEEK LATER, COLLINS picked Mackinnon up from outside his block of flats in the Docklands. They were both starting another week of earlies.

"Did you put your application in for MIT?" Mackinnon asked as Collins pulled into Lime Street.

"No. I thought I'd leave it a while. I reckon I should enjoy the quiet life for a bit longer." Collins indicated and turned right into the heavy morning traffic.

"Maybe you're right," Mackinnon said, thinking about his own application.

The Roger Cleeves case made Mackinnon think long and hard about whether he was really cut out for this job, whether he could cope with the fact that cases like these never really left you. Building the case against Roger Cleeves would take months. Maybe after that, after the bastard was locked up, Mackinnon's anger would fade.

Maybe the sickening images that seemed to be imprinted on his brain would go away, too. He hoped so.

Roger Cleeves had spilled his guts and admitted he'd taken seven girls from the Star Academy so they could take part in some sort of twisted competition. In his mind, he was some sort of Svengali figure and the girls had been his performers until he'd grown tired of them.

He killed five young women by smashing open their skulls with a hammer he'd taken from one of Fred Oakland's basement storerooms. He killed poor Henryk Blonski the same way, and he would have killed Anya and Victoria too, eventually.

In a series of harrowing interviews, Anya told them how Cleeves made them perform for him. The winner was allowed to live, but her prize was to witness the horrific murder of her competitor. It really was a competition to the death.

Roger Cleeves insisted his son knew nothing about the abductions, but Mackinnon wasn't convinced. In his head, Roger and Nathan Cleeves had merged into one person. He hated them both. That was another reason to wonder if he was really suited to this job. Could you really be a police officer and feel hatred this strong? How did you live with that?

"What did you get up to this weekend?" Collins asked, breaking Mackinnon's train of thought.

Mackinnon grimaced. "Spent it with Chloe and her daughters."

"You really like her, don't you?"

Mackinnon settled back in the passenger seat. "I want it

to work out. But what the hell do I know about teenage girls?"

Collins grinned. "Last week we faced down a knife-wielding serial-killer, and now you're scared of a couple of teenage girls?"

"You haven't met them," Mackinnon said. "They're scary."

"No one would believe it to look at you Jack, but you're a big girl's blouse."

"Shut up and drive, Collins," Mackinnon said, trying not to smile. "Just shut up and drive."

EXTRACT FROM DEADLY MOTIVE

Ted Sanders crept along Parks Road, keeping to the shadows. It was eleven pm and quiet, but he knew he needed to avoid the spying eyes of the surveillance cameras.

When he reached the junction, he stood still for a few moments and tried to slow his breathing. He needed to be calm tonight.

He lowered his bag onto the pavement, circled his shoulder to relieve the ache and felt the blood tingle back into his arm.

He looked towards the University of Oxford's science area. Sandstone university buildings decorated with grimacing grotesques lined the road. The perfect image for a tourist postcard of Oxford.

But not for long.

Ted saw his target on the opposite side of the road and smiled. He pulled the hood of his sweatshirt forward to hide his face. He had chosen the navy-blue, hooded sweatshirt and black jeans so he could blend into the darkness.

A friend told him the university had installed an extra twenty security cameras when they started construction on the new animal house. Ted knew where they were.

He crouched down and snatched up the carrier bag. He needed to get on with it. Tonight, timing was everything.

Looking down, he saw a deep red stain on the pavement. He felt a stab of fear.

Evidence.

He lifted the bag and scowled at the red liquid oozing from a hole in the plastic. Some spilt on his hand, and he rubbed it between his thumb and forefinger. It felt sticky.

He saw red splashes on his trainers. He looked behind him to the path he had taken along Parks Road. He knew he had left a telltale trail. It didn't matter. No one would notice it tonight in the dark.

A sharp cry carried over the night air and Ted stopped to listen.

Although the protest should have been over hours ago, chants from animal rights protesters echoed in the distance. That meant some of the protesters were hanging around on the outskirts of the science area, but they wouldn't interfere. The university had an injunction that banned them getting too close to the science area.

They wouldn't even see Ted tonight.

He turned right into South Parks Road and passed the Dyson Perrins Laboratory and the Inorganic Chemistry building on his left. The old buildings stood tall. Blue plaques on their walls detailed their history and listed the names of scientists who had worked there.

Tonight, he had no interest in these historic buildings. Tonight, he was heading to one of the newest buildings in the area.

The Chemistry Research Laboratory stood opposite the older science departments. It looked as if it had been constructed entirely of glass. The red brick Dyson Perrins Laboratory, on the opposite side of the road, reflected in its dark glass walls.

His friend, Alex, worked in the huge glass building and had kept Ted supplied with information. Some details were more useful than others. He told Ted about the high security involved when the Queen attended the official opening of the glass building last year.

Ted stared at the stark, cube-shaped building. He wondered what the Queen thought of it. According to Alex, the building had won an architectural award, but it was a perfect example of the type of architecture Prince Charles hated, which was almost enough to make Ted like it.

But all that had nothing to do with why he was here tonight.

Ted had chosen this building because it stood on the corner of Mansfield Road, directly opposite the construction site for the new animal house.

Hoarding and a high, spiked, steel fence surrounded the site. He would not be able to get anywhere near it. It would be stupid to even try; and even if he could, what would be the point? No one would be able to see his work through the barriers.

Security was tightly controlled at the site and the entrance opened only twice a day for the construction workers and trucks transporting the building materials. He had watched them for weeks, plotting and waiting for the perfect opportunity.

The construction workers turned up every morning, wearing balaclavas to hide their faces while they worked. They were ashamed of their involvement.

But not ashamed enough.

Alex assured him the chemistry department did not use animals in any of their laboratories, but Ted didn't think that would weaken his message. It was still a university building, after all, and the side facing the new animal house had an expansive white wall. A blank canvas. Everyone who saw it would understand his message.

Ted crouched at the side of the building. He wanted to make sure no one could see him from inside.

The lights from one of the labs shone down over the courtyard. Someone was working late. The labs had motion-sensing lights that switched off automatically when the lab was empty.

He felt a line of sweat travel down to the small of his back. He hadn't planned on this. The labs were supposed to be empty.

But the occupied lab was on the top floor, so it was unlikely they would see or hear him, and a security check usually took place at midnight, which meant he couldn't wait.

He would have to take a chance and do it now.

* * *

Inside the Chemistry Research Laboratory, Ruby Wei

walked into the lab's write-up area, waving her arms wildly over her head to trigger the lights.

The motion-sensing lights were part of the new chemistry building's eco-drive: if there was no one in the room, there was no need to waste electricity on lights. This worked fine during the day when lots of people were in the lab, but at night when it was quiet, the lights would turn off if you sat still for more than five minutes.

A split second after her manic arm-waving, the lights flickered back on. She pulled a chair up to her computer and logged into her email account. She was supposed to be writing up an experiment, while her cells were incubating, but she couldn't concentrate.

She stared at the computer screen. She needed to reply to her father's email, but she had to choose her words carefully. Over the last few weeks, she hadn't been calling or emailing her parents as regularly as usual.

Her parents had sent an email, saying they understood it was because she was so busy in the lab trying to finish her PhD.

It wasn't true. Well, maybe it was partly true; she was nearing the end of her project. But if she were honest, she avoided speaking to her parents because she didn't know how to tell them she wasn't coming back to China. At least not yet.

Ruby stood up, yawned and walked between two desks towards the huge windows that ran along the edge of the laboratory and overlooked South Parks Road.

What was that? A movement? Was someone out there?

She stared out into the darkness.

The bright fluorescent strip lights inside the laboratory made it difficult to see anything outside. The orange glow of the street lamps looked dull in comparison.

She stood by the window for a moment, looking at her own ghostly reflection staring back at her, and pressed a hand to her chest. She could feel her heart thumping.

She waited until she was absolutely sure there was no one out there. She was imagining things. The protests against the new animal house had made her nervous; that was all.

She turned away from the window and glanced back at the computer screen. She had to find the courage to tell her parents that she wanted to stay in Oxford.

Ruby had left China aged sixteen, and she had studied for her A-levels, her degree and now her DPhil in the UK. As each year passed, she became more attached to her adopted country and less connected to her homeland. That didn't mean she never wanted to go back. She would go home someday. There were things she missed.

Since leaving China eight years ago, she had been home only once, to spend Chinese New Year with her relatives. It had been a wonderful trip, and she enjoyed visiting her extended family and telling everyone about her life in the UK, but it was just a trip, which was very different from going back permanently.

Of course, she loved her parents, and she knew her parents loved her. They were extremely proud of their only child's achievements. They loved her, but they didn't really understand her.

A year or so into her DPhil at Oxford, over video chat,

she tried to explain to her parents an exciting result she had found in her research. She had been working on a human protein and trying to discover its structure. In the lab, they'd used a method where they grew crystals of her protein and bombarded it with X-rays.

The pattern of the diffracted X-rays were then analysed by computer, using all kinds of complicated mathematics, which, if Ruby was honest, she didn't fully understand yet. Then, just weeks later, to Ruby's amazement, she sat in front of her computer screen and saw the loops, the ribbons and the perfect helices that made this protein.

She just sat there for ages, staring at it, mesmerised by the idea that, although this protein existed in the blood of every single living person, she was the very first person to see it.

At that moment, no one else in the world knew what it looked like.

When she tried to describe the feeling to her parents, there was an awkward pause before her father asked if that meant she would get a good grade.

Soon, she would be able to tell them about the post-doctoral position she hoped to get, working in Dr. O'Connor's laboratory. She hoped he would confirm it this week so she could tell her parents that she had a good job lined up.

Good career prospects were important to her parents, and the job offer might soften the blow when she told them she wanted to stay in Oxford.

Ruby glanced at the window again. Working at this time of night gave her the creeps. The fact that no one could enter the building unless they had an access card was reassuring, but that didn't mean there wasn't someone lurking around after the protest this afternoon.

She shivered.

* * *

When the light directly in front of him flickered on, Ted froze.

His muscles tensed, ready to run, but he forced himself to stay crouched on the floor. The light came from a ground floor lab, only a few feet away.

He felt his breath quicken as he squinted towards the lab and realised he recognised the person who had triggered the lights.

Ruby Wei, the Chinese student in the same research group as Alex, stood silhouetted by the window and was staring straight at him.

Ted pushed his body back against the wall, away from the light. The darkness should protect him. If he stayed still, she probably wouldn't recognise him or even see him.

She just stood there, staring out of the window. Had she spotted him?

If she had seen him, she would have shown some reaction by now. Almost a minute passed before she moved away from the glass. He watched her walk away from the window and pick up a white lab coat.

Why was she in the lab at this time of night? Didn't she have a life?

He glanced at his watch; he had to get on with it because

security would be here soon. He took a deep breath and then smiled.

He would do it now, right under the silly cow's nose.

* * *

Thanks for reading. If you want to read the rest, Deadly Motive is available now.

THANK YOU!

THANKS FOR READING DEADLY Obsession. I hope you enjoyed it!

Would you like to know when my next book is available? You can sign up for my new release email at www.dsbutlerbooks.com/newsletter

You can follow me on Twitter at @dsbutler, or like my Facebook page at http://facebook.com/dsbutler.author.

Reviews are like gold to authors. They spread the word and help readers find books. Please leave a review if you have the time.

ALSO BY D. S. BUTLER

Deadly Obsession

Deadly Motive

Deadly Revenge

Deadly Justice

Deadly Ritual

Deadly Payback

Deadly Game

Lost Child

Her Missing Daughter

Bring Them Home

Where Secrets Lie

If you would like to be informed when the next book is released, sign up for the newsletter:

http://www.dsbutlerbooks.com/newsletter/

Written as Dani Oakley

East End Trouble

East End Diamond

East End Retribution

ACKNOWLEDGMENTS

MANY PEOPLE HELPED TO provide ideas and background for this book. My thanks and gratitude to DI Dave Carter and Richard Searle for generously sharing their time and wealth of experience.

My thanks, too, to all the people who read the first drafts of the Deadly Series and gave helpful suggestions – in particular Joan, Therese, Maureen and Rhona. And to Chris, who, as always, supported me.

Made in the USA
Monee, IL
06 October 2020

44078624R00146